STOLEN SALVATION

SHADOW ELITE BOOK 4

MADDIE WADE

Stolen Salvation
Shadow Elite Book Four
By Maddie Wade

Published by Maddie Wade
Copyright © July 2022

Cover: Clem Parsons-Metatec
Editing: Black Opal Editing
Formatting: Black Opal Editing

First edition July 2022 ©Maddie Wade

Acknowledgments

I am so lucky to have such an amazing team around me without which I could never bring my books to life. I am so grateful to have you in my life, you are more than friends you are so essential to my life.

My wonderful beta team, Greta, and Deanna who are brutally honest and beautifully kind. If it is rubbish you tell me, it is and if you love it you are effusive. Your support means so much to me.

My editor—Linda at Black Opal Editing, who is so patient. She is so much more than an editor, she is a teacher and a friend.

Thank you to my group Maddie's Minxes, your support and love for Fortis, Eidolon, Ryoshi and now Shadow Elite you are so important to me. Special thanks to Rowena, Tracey, Faith, Rachel, Carolyn, Kellie, Maria, Rochelle, Becky, Vicky, Greta, Deanna, Sharon and Linda L for making the group such a friendly place to be.

My UK PA Clem Parsons who listens to all my ramblings and helps me every single day.

My ARC Team for not keeping me on edge too long while I wait for feedback.

Lastly and most importantly thank you to my readers who have embraced my books so wholeheartedly and shown a love for the stories in my head. To hear you say that you see my characters as family makes me so humble and proud. I hope you enjoy Bishop and Charlie's love story as much as I did.

Cover: Clem Parsons @Metatec
Editing: Black Opal Editing

PROLOGUE

B<small>LOOD BLOOMED ON HIS SHOULDER, AND</small> C<small>HARLIE FELT NAUSEA STIR IN HER</small> belly, but it was the look of utter shock and betrayal on his face that shredded her heart into tiny pieces. She'd just shot the only man she'd ever loved. Lowering her weapon, she fought the urge to go to him, to help him and beg him to forgive her, to listen to her reasons, but none of them mattered. That single shot had ended any chance she might have of a happy ever after with him. Hell, with anyone. Nobody compared to Noah Bishop, they never had from the second they'd met years ago. From that day to this, it had been the two of them against the world.

But the world had won, tearing them apart and making a mockery of the vows they'd made to each other. To love, honour, and defend, in sickness and in health. How cruel that she was doing all those things as she watched him bleed, his wound allowing blood to seep from him.

"Come, Lottie, it's time for us to leave."

Cocking her head to the powerful and deadly man behind her, she set her jaw to stop the snarl edging up her throat. He needed to believe she was who she said she was, or they'd both die. "Coming, Armand."

Her voice held an adoring quality, the falseness obvious to her and anyone who knew her, but this man had more ego than anyone she'd ever met. It was what made him so dangerous. She had to stop him, but she'd never wanted it to go down this way or for her husband, the man she loved, to end up as collateral damage.

Shifting the white dress so it didn't swish through the blood at her feet, she crouched as if picking up her designer clutch. Laying a hand on Noah's arm, she watched his eyes flicker open, pain from the earlier beating Armand and his men had given him already making him weak. "I'm so sorry."

A strong hand gripped her wrist and she blinked away tears. "Don't do this, Charlie."

Pain echoed through her heart, shattering her in such a way she knew she'd never be whole again. "I'm sorry, I don't have a choice."

"We always have a choice."

His voice was laced with pain, gritty and weak and she knew he'd fall unconscious soon and she needed to be gone when he did. "You're wrong."

Ripping her arm from his grip, she hated that the last time he touched her would be etched on her soul with the betrayal in his eyes. His head fell back, and he looked away as if her face caused him pain and distaste.

As she straightened her back and walked away, head held high, she knew that Noah would never know how hard this was for her or how her world had shattered that night. He'd hate her but she'd saved him, and that was all that mattered.

Voices all around him seeped through the thick fog of pain in his chest, not from the beating or the bullet but from the betrayal he'd never expected. Charlie, his sweet Charlie, who still put out cookies and milk for Santa even as an adult because she'd missed out as a child. She was the absolute love of his life and she'd crushed that love under her dainty-heeled foot. His will to live and fight past this felt like it had been sucked out of him as she'd wrenched her arm out of his grasp and walked away, taking her excuses with her.

Large hands touched his shoulder, and he didn't even have the energy to flinch.

"He's lost a lot of blood. Let's get a line in and get some fluids going."

Bishop felt his body being lifted and wished they'd just let him die. He tried to articulate the words but whatever they'd put in his IV was making his tongue feel thick and his brain unfocused and black.

Maybe the blackness that beckoned was better anyway. He didn't want to remember all the ways his life had gone to shit. Or the way Charlie smiled every Christmas morning when she came downstairs to find he'd eaten the cookies and drunk the milk she'd left. Or the way she'd thank him later, her body a sensual delight he'd never been able to resist.

Bishop jolted, his body slamming upright as bright light hit his eyes. His gaze shooting around the room, he took in the bed, the white walls, the incessant sounds of beeping, and the sterile scent of antiseptic. Lifting his hand, he saw the IV and the white gown he was wearing, and everything flooded back to him. Charlie shooting him, the look in her eyes, and then the pain as she walked away, leaving him for dead.

"You gave us quite the scare, Mr Bishop."

Bishop turned his head toward the deep voice and saw a man leaning against the wall, his arms folded over his chest, his intent stare taking in every nuance of Bishop's reaction. He was tall, well over six feet, with dark hair and blue eyes. Muscular, and aware of every single sound in the room, he had operator written all over him and Bishop knew exactly who he was.

"Jack Granger, to what do I owe this visit?" Bishop motioned toward himself with his hand, the IV feeling uncomfortable. "I'm not really up for saving the world with you right now."

Granger pushed off the wall and moved slowly across the room to take the seat beside him meant for visitors. The place where loved ones would wait, with worry etched on their faces for the person they loved to wake up. Bitterness, hot and nauseous slid up his throat making his head pound. He had nobody. But then he hadn't had anyone he could count on for a long time, not until Charlie and now she'd proven his worth was shit.

"I came to offer you a job."

Bishop thought the drugs might be affecting him more than he thought because he was sure Granger had just offered him a job. "Are you shitting me?"

Granger coughed to hide the smirk. "No, not shitting you. We found you beaten, shot, and left for dead by MI5. I figured you might be up for a new challenge, and I have a proposition for you."

Despite everything, Bishop was intrigued. Granger was right, he had no intention of going back to his job at MI5. Not for the reasons Granger probably thought, but because he couldn't cope with the reminders of Charlie. They'd worked every mission as a team. Even though the higher-ups didn't like it, they tolerated them together because they always got the job done.

No, he couldn't do that without her. It would be like a knife to his heart every time he spoke to one of his contacts and had to explain that she was no longer working with him. To see the looks of pity on the faces of the people they worked with. He'd always known he wasn't good enough for her. That she was a wonder, a beautiful light in a world of darkness and far too good for the likes of him. Looked like she'd come to the same conclusion.

"I'm listening."

Granger seemed pleased, his shoulders leaning forward just the slightest bit. "I'm putting together a team of men and women who'll live and work together for the most part. Your old life will be erased from any database, and you'll cease to exist. Whether you walk out of here alive, or we tell the world you're dead is up to you, but all records of you will be gone. The team will answer to a lead who'll answer to me. It will be autonomous and highly secretive."

"That's fine, I have nobody in my life but don't put me down as dead." No matter how much he now hated the woman he'd loved, he didn't want her to believe she'd killed him. Some small part of him still cared and he hated himself for the weakness. Focusing back on what Granger had said he asked, "What will this team do?"

"There are far too many instances where red tape and politics allow injustice to happen and for dangerous people to go back into positions of power. We'll cut through that tape and handle it. There'll also be occasions where we travel abroad to take out threats that nobody has the balls to handle. We'll let them carry on twisting their pearls in worry over the consequences while we actually deal with it."

Bishop considered Granger's words. He knew the man to be a good operator and that he worked directly for the Monarchy but not the details of him or his team. It seemed he had more power than anyone realised, even MI5. "Why me?"

Granger cocked his head, his hands hanging loosely between his knees. "You're one of the best in your field. You have an excellent close and success rate on your cases and an impressive list of assets. We need someone like you, and I think you'd be a good fit for our team."

"Tell me more about them?"

Granger paused and seemed to consider his words. "Some of them are people who've led a pretty grey life according to the law and then there are others who've just damn right broken it. But they've done so for the right reasons or because of a path they were put on that they couldn't get off without some help. We offered that help, and they give us the knowledge and resources we need. Others are former special forces who fell afoul of the leadership. It's a mixed bag, but they're all good people at heart and want to help. They're highly skilled and will be the best of the best by the time we finish training them."

"Who's the leader you mentioned?"

"A man named Niall O'Scanlan, but you might know him as Bás. He, along with a woman named Nadia Benassi, known as Duchess, will lead this team."

Bishop had heard of them both and they were like night and day, but Granger wasn't lying about their backgrounds or the skills they had.

"I take it once you walk out the door the offer goes with you?"

Granger smirked. "You know the drill, Bishop."

He leaned his head back against the pillows and considered his options. He had fuck all to lose and maybe a challenge and purpose would stop him from swallowing a bullet, which had been the first thought in his head when Charlie walked away.

Rolling his head on the pillow, he looked at Granger who was cool and controlled. No emotion on his face in the slightest. He was used to working with people like Granger, who cut to the chase and showed nothing to the outside world. "I have one stipulation."

"What is it?"

"I want Armand Vernier dead."

Bishop didn't have it in him to harm a hair on Charlie's head but the man she'd left with, who she'd gotten mixed up with, needed to die.

Granger dipped his chin, as he leaned back and crossed his ankles. "I can agree to that, but you won't be part of the mission. I won't have revenge getting in the way of this team. Eidolon will handle him."

"I can live with that."

Granger smiled and stood abruptly, forcing Bishop to wonder where the hell he was because this sure as hell wasn't an NHS hospital. "Hey, where the hell am I?"

Granger smirked. "At my headquarters. You took quite the

beating and Dr Decker spent four hours trying to dig that bullet out of you while you kept trying to die."

"From the bullet wound?"

"No, internal bleeding from the beating. The bullet was more of a deep scratch."

Bishop shook his head, a grin twisting his lips at the thought a bullet in the shoulder would be considered a scratch. "How long have I been out?"

"Two days all told." Granger pointed at him. "Get some rest and recuperate because once training starts you're going to wish for death. I want this team to live and breathe in tandem."

"I won't let you down, Jack, and thanks."

"I know you won't and don't thank me yet. You might regret handing your life over."

"No, I won't. I have nothing left for me in my old life."

Granger offered him a closed expression as if he wanted to say something, but he kept his mouth shut, and nodded. Which left Bishop to contemplate his future, one without the other half of his heart.

Charlie had ripped his heart out and stamped on it, turning on him in a way he'd never seen coming. Well, that would never happen again. He'd never trust another person with his heart like that. Charlie was dead to him and so was the love they'd shared. It had been an illusion and he had no place for it in his life going forward.

This was a new start, and he'd be the best he could be for his new team. The past was just that, dead and gone.

CHAPTER 1

Mɪsᴛ sᴇᴛᴛʟᴇᴅ ʟɪᴋᴇ ᴀ ᴄᴏᴏʟ ʙʟᴀɴᴋᴇᴛ ᴏᴠᴇʀ ᴛʜᴇ Bʟᴀᴄᴋ Mᴏᴜɴᴛᴀɪɴs ᴀs Bɪsʜᴏᴘ lay flat on his belly in the damp moss. The sound of a Kestrel flying overhead, searching the ground for prey, reached his ears. Blinking through the scope of his rifle he surveyed the land, looking for something out of place, a sign that one of his team members was close. The scent of moss and grass mixed with the smell of the sheep shit all around him from the hundreds of wild, roaming flock.

These exercises were some of his favourites, allowing him to get out and be free while honing his skills as an operator against some of, if not *the* best, operators in the world. Split into two teams, Shadow spent hours and hours on these mountains, practising patience, tracking, and the art of survival against the deadliest foe: the elements.

He knew Hurricane was on the opposite ridge, watching for the same signs as he was. Snow was the kidnapped victim this time as Bás, Bein, Reaper, Lotus, and Watchdog worked against his team. Titan and Duchess were closing in on the formation of rocks where they suspected Snow was being held.

A click on his comms unit signalled they were correct. Silently moving across the space, his body close to the ground, he zeroed in on their position, knowing Hurricane was covering his back from any attack.

Ducking low, he could see Duchess and Titan, and more importantly, he could see Reaper who was guarding Snow. His camouflage was good, only the tiny golden blond of his hair that wasn't covered in paint gave away his position. Taking aim, he watched his friend in his cross hairs turn his head as if sensing eyes on him and look directly at the scope. Before Reaper could react, Bishop took the shot and watched as red paint bloomed on his friend's chest. Reaper went down, but the job wasn't over, they still had to rescue Snow without getting shot by any of the other team members and Bein was still out there. He was the one Bishop knew would be the hardest to find. Growing up in the Highlands meant the mountains and woods had been his childhood playground.

As he moved in, Duchess took down Bás but got shot by Lotus.

"Bishop, watch your right flank."

Titan's warning came as Bein fired. The paint skimmed his leg as he rolled, but it wouldn't be a fatal shot, more of a scratch as Jack had once called his shoulder wound. Shaking that thought away he fired back, missing as his teammate seemed to have vanished into thin air.

"Damn it, where is he?"

"Titan is down. Watchdog took him out."

"Fuck."

Bishop jogged towards Snow and almost got his ass bitten by Scout who ran at him, closely followed by Valentina.

Thankfully, Snow had taken things into her own hands and gotten free. She took down Lotus with a shot of yellow paint to the chest as Val called Scout back.

Bishop tagged Snow and the exercise was over.

He rolled to his back panting, a giant smile on his face from the exhilaration of the chase and being alive.

There had been a long time when he would've given anything to have died the night his ex-wife shot him, but he was finally starting to live again, thanks to these people around him.

Valentina stood over him with her hand out and a smile on her face. "Scout almost nailed you."

Bishop took her hand and allowed her to pull him up as he frowned. "I can't believe you were going to let him bite me in the ass."

Val shrugged. "All's fair in love and war, Bish."

"Yeah, well, the losing team buys the drinks tonight."

Val glanced behind her at Bás. "Hey, Bás, Bishop says the round's on you."

Bás sent a middle finger salute and Watchdog burst out laughing as they packed up and cleaned any trace of them being there from the mountain.

"If Bás opens his wallet, moths will escape."

Bás pointed at Watchdog. "Just for that, you can buy the first round, dickwad."

Watchdog smirked. "Yes, boss man."

The rest of the day was spent with him manning the front desk of the Mountain Rescue Centre which was a front for Shadow. They did do mountain rescues on occasion and had made wonderful friends in this village. As he closed the doors for the night, he flipped the phones to auto, so any calls to the number would go through to Watchdog and headed out.

The local pub was a fifteen-minute walk, and he knew some of his friends would already be there. Sucking in the cooling air of the early spring evening, he relished the longer evenings now the clocks had sprung forward.

Stepping into the familiar surroundings of The Crown public house, it felt like coming home. A fire was burning in the grate, he could hear laughter and friends chatting, the scent of homecooked food that came from the back, and the smell of hops and beer.

Nodding at Bob the landlord, who knew what and who the team were and was talking with old man Johnson, he ordered a pint of IPA from the bar and saw Watchdog waving him toward the table they'd commandeered in the corner.

The villagers were used to them all now, but they hadn't always given them such a warm welcome. A small village like this one didn't take kindly to newcomers until they got the measure of them.

Taking his drink, he walked over and sat with his back to the door, knowing his friends would always have his six. "We eating?"

Titan flipped the beer mat in his fingers as he responded. "Hell, yes, I'm starving."

"You're always starving." Hurricane threw a peanut at Titan who caught it like some freaking wizard.

"You boys are truly just overgrown children, aren't you?" Lotus was shaking her head in disgust at the two men.

"Nothing wrong with that, Miss Uppity Pants."

"Oh, mature, Titan. Real mature."

Bishop zoned them out as he began chatting with Watchdog about a program, but felt someone come up behind him, and an old, ringed hand landed on his shoulder.

"My boys, I'd like you to meet my mother."

Bishop swivelled in his chair to take in Mrs Jones, who was seventy if she was a day, and beside her was an older woman who barely made it to her shoulders she was so tiny. Jumping to his feet, he offered Mrs Jones and her mother a seat as Titan did the same.

Wizened eyes looked up at him with a twinkle as Mrs Jones' mother took the seat. "Thank you, son."

"Mum, this is Bishop and Titan and their friends." Mrs Jones looked up at him. "She wanted to come and meet you specifically."

"It's a pleasure to meet you, Mrs—?"

"Howard, but you can call me Rose."

"Well, Rose, it's my pleasure."

He kissed her hand and heard her cackle with glee. "Oh, you're a charmer but you hide so much pain. You need to forgive, Noah."

His blood ran cold at her words. Nobody called him Noah except his ex, and she was long out of the picture. "I don't hold grudges, Miss Rose."

An aged, wrinkled hand grasped his with more strength than he'd expected. "Dear heart, you do, and it's ill placed. You need to forgive if you're going to heal the rift with your other half."

Bishop looked at Mrs Jones for help and she smiled. "Mum is somewhat of a psychic."

Bishop relaxed, his shoulders dropping from the state of tension they'd been in when she spoke her warning. "Ah."

"You don't believe?"

Bishop angled his head to Rose. "I didn't say that. I'm just more of a sceptic."

"That's okay, son, you'll see. Your destiny is bringing the past and future together."

"Okay."

"You'll see."

"So, Miss Rose, are you here long?"

The old woman pursed her lips and frowned at her daughter. "Damn girl made me come live with her so she can take care of me like I'm a child needing my nappy changed. I'm a God damn grown woman. Been through a war, worked the land, and raised my babies when my husband, God rest his soul, was killed in action. I don't need a babysitter."

Bishop rolled his lips to keep from smiling. He loved her feisty spirit, even if her words from earlier terrified him slightly. "Maybe she just wants you close. Maybe she needs you, not the other way around."

"Hm, maybe you're right, young man. Perhaps this whole village needs me, and especially you young-uns."

"Well, I, for one, will look forward to seeing you around the village."

Miss Rose winked. "If I was twenty years younger, I'd be chasing you around this here mountain."

Bishop winked back. "And I'd let you, Miss Rose."

Her cackle made him laugh out loud, the surprise turn of the evening making him smile. Miss Rose left shortly after, and the team managed to get a food order in before most of them headed back to the compound. Then it was just him and Watchdog drinking by the fire.

"What are your thoughts on Duchess and this case with Cavendish?"

Bishop cocked his head as he considered Watchdog's question. He'd learned early on his friend never asked anything just for the sake of it. He always had a reason, and that he was asking about Duchess was telling.

Taking a sip of his beer, he bought himself a minute to consider what his thoughts were. She'd been working on this case for over a year now and it was weighing heavily on her. As the time went on and she worked with Gideon and Damon Cavendish to expose their younger brother and find the evidence to convict him, she'd looked more and more tired.

"I think it's coming to a turning point and Duchess has more going on than she's telling us."

Watchdog's lips turned down. "I agree. I'm worried about her."

"You spoken to Bás about it?"

"Not yet."

"You should. I think we all need pulling in on this soon if we're going to work the Project Cradle case actively."

Project Cradle was an old CIA initiative from the nineties that involved taking female babies from willing mothers and training them and educating them from birth to be assets of the US Government. It had been shut down, but a rogue agent had taken it private and now the mothers were not willing in any way. It made his blood boil to even think about.

"That's the thing. I can't find evidence of Carter being involved."

"You sure he's involved? Cradle started long before his time. Unless his father was involved."

"Or his mother."

"That's possible, I guess. She is the driving force behind her son's criminal empire."

"It doesn't make sense to me how a mother could push her son into that kind of shit."

Bishop drained his glass. "That's because you had a mother who adored you."

Watchdog seemed to get lost in thought at those words. "Yeah, I did."

Silence swept over them as each man considered their past. Watchdog's life had been very different from his own. Where his parents had died, Watchdog's mother had been the kind every child dreamed of until Alzheimer's stole her away at just fifty-six. Now her son was a stranger to her and the boy she'd supported was a man making a difference to those around him, and they had no clue.

"Uh, Bish?"

The wariness in Watchdog's voice made him stiffen slightly, the sudden feeling of being watched making his spine straighten. "Yes?"

"You have eyes on you."

"Is she blonde, gorgeous, and looks like she could kick your ass?"

"Yep, that's her."

"Fuck."

CHAPTER 2

HER PALMS FELT SWEATY AS SHE WALKED INTO THE CROWN PUB AND CAST her eyes around the dark space. With a low ceiling, brass taps on the dark wood bar and burgundy velvet on the barstools. It was a quintessential British Pub, right down to the wary looks shot at her from the locals who leaned on the bar talking.

Rubbing her hands on her jean-clad legs she tried to infuse her usual calm into the nerves spinning cartwheels in her belly. He was just a man, this was just a conversation, but that was a lie and one she had never had any luck believing. Noah Bishop was more than that to her. For most of her adult life, he'd been her everything and in her heart, he still was.

Her gaze stuttered as it swept over the man she'd come to find. His hair was lighter than she remembered it, probably from the time he'd spent in the Australian sunshine with his friend. The usual dark blond was ashier in colour now, but still spiked and messy in a way that made her think of running her fingers through it as he pounded into her body.

He was tall, around six feet even, his lean strength quiet and subtle, like a panther coiled and ready for a fight, but not actively looking for trouble. A smile tipped her lips as she thought of all the people who'd underestimated him because of his friendly demeanour, and the hours she'd spent running her hands over that muscular frame, her fingers and mouth not able to get enough of his sinfully sexy body. A painful vision of him letting another woman touch him filled her and she swallowed the nausea that thought evoked. She deserved it for letting him go, for walking away when she should've held tight.

A new scar on his cheekbone made her belly ache, pain heavy in her chest with regret as he smiled at the friend who sat next to him. His brown eyes lit up at whatever had been said between them.

Charlie took a seat at the bar and ordered a drink from the bartender who watched her warily. He was former SAS, and she knew he knew about Shadow, the team Noah now worked for. Sipping her sparkling water, she saw the second Noah sensed her eyes on him. His watchful gaze swept across the room and landed on her with dislike that quickly turned to open hostility on his face.

She'd known when she'd done what she had two years ago that he'd never forgive her. Having no choice was a weak excuse in his eyes. Seeing the hatred he felt towards her and hearing the way he called her she-devil hurt more than it should. Looking back on the night she'd thrown her life away, Charlie always wished she could go back and make different choices.

Noah had every right to hate her, and she had no right to do what she was about to do, and that was to ask for his help.

She kept eye contact as he drained his beer and spoke to his male friend, one she hadn't met at the scene of Princess Lucía's home a few months ago. Perhaps he was the tech genius they all spoke of as if he was a genuine god.

His controlled gaze pinned her to her seat and even as Charlie felt the negativity radiating from him, she couldn't stop the rush of love she still felt for him. He came to stand beside her, his familiar after-shave making her tummy drop like lead as memories washed over her. It was a scent she'd picked out for him, one that turned her body to molten lava.

Closing her eyes, she chased the past away and concentrated on the man in front of her.

Noah had trained his whole career to blend in and be the grey man, to her though, he stood out, catching her attention with his sexy smirk and the way he had of speaking to someone as if nobody else existed in that moment. Focused and intent, as if what a person said mattered more than anything in the world to him.

"What do you want, Charlie?"

No hello or common courtesy. He didn't want her there and he was making that abundantly clear. His accent had less of the northern roundness to it, and she missed it. So many people underestimated him because of that friendly tone, and many had lived to regret it. The others had died.

"What, no friendly 'how are you, what you been up to'?" She couldn't help herself, the hurt piercing her from his curt greeting.

He leaned an arm on the bar and cocked his head toward her. "You've got to be fucking kidding me, right?"

Charlie bristled, her usual careful friendly demeanour bruised, and she had nobody to blame but herself. "I know it didn't work out with us, Noah, but there's no need to be rude."

His eyebrows rose. "Didn't work out? You fucking shot me and left me for dead. That's hardly an amicable breakup."

Charlie dropped her head, shame washing over her and yet she'd done what she had to save him. She'd never tell him that because he'd never believe her. Glancing up, she saw his friend openly staring now, Noah's dislike reflected on his face too. They all hated her but she had to push through and do what she'd come to do. "I know and I'm sorry, I truly am."

Noah held up his hand, his handsome face so familiar and yet he wasn't the man she'd fallen in love with. She'd changed him, taken away the crinkle in the corners of his eyes when he looked at her as if he was constantly on the cusp of smiling when she was around. Now a frown shared space with distrust.

"Save it. I don't want to hear it. Just tell me what you want. Because we both know this isn't a social call."

If only he knew how many times she'd wanted to reach out to him for that very reason, to just talk to him, to ask him how he was and beg him to forgive her. It was a cliché, but Noah had been her best friend as well as her husband. When they'd split it hadn't just been the sex she missed but also her best friend.

Charlie shook her head. "No, it isn't. Is there somewhere we can talk?"

Noah sighed as if bored with this already and she fought the urge to turn tail and run from the anguish flooding her.

"In here."

Noah motioned toward a back room, his head lifting toward the bar manager who acknowledged the silent request with a nod. Her arm brushed his chest in the tight space and sparks of desire shot through her blood. In the small space, his scent felt heady, like a drug and her mind went to all the times she'd found that scent on their sheets and heat bloomed inside her. She would never admit it, but she had a bottle of his cologne and would spritz her pillow with it when she was feeling exceptionally lonely.

Noah stepped back as if burned, quickly putting distance between them like she was a leper and he might catch something. Charlie ducked her head so he wouldn't see the hurt on her face at his action. The small back room held an old wooden desk with chips along the edge, a metal filing cabinet, and a kitchen chair being used as a desk chair. The magnolia walls were yellowed from years of use. It was serviceable and private, just what she'd asked for. Steeling her spine she thought of what she had to do and why she'd come. This wasn't about her; this was about Andrea.

"Out with it."

His impatience and obvious dislike made her temper snap. "Bloody hell, Noah, when did you get so impatient?"

"When my wife shot me."

His glare made something break inside her and she moved to push past him. "Forget it."

His hand on her biceps stilled her as he dropped his head. "Charlie, wait."

This close she could see the amber flecks in his eyes, the stubble on his jaw and her hands itched to touch him, to kiss the scar that was new. His lips were so close she only had to lean in slightly to savour the familiar taste of him. Electricity buzzed around them as the outside world seemed to still, enclosing them in a bubble that was timeless, with no guilt or past to cloud them.

God, she wanted him to kiss her, to make her feel the way only he could, to tell her he forgave her and still loved her. A crash outside the door, glass smashing and then the sound of someone cursing, broke the spell and he released her, moving back.

"What do you need?"

Charlie took a few breaths to get her equilibrium in order and store her feelings away for another day. Leaning against the desk she crossed her ankles and folded her arms to hide her erect nipples from his knowing gaze. His eyes skimmed her, and she realised it was too late, he'd seen the effect he had on her.

Powering through she did what she came here for. "Andrea is missing. She was at Uni in Manchester doing her master's in design. A few weeks ago she called me crying to say she was pregnant and didn't know what to do. I was in Prague at the time and couldn't get back, but when I did, I went to see her, and she was gone. According to her roommate, she quit college, some guy came and packed her stuff, and she was gone. I've tried everything to find her, reached out to sources, and spoken to her friends. I even called my dad, who just berated me down the phone for letting this happen."

"Dick."

Charlie smiled; Noah had always hated her father. "Yeah, he hasn't changed. Anyway, the only lead I have is that she was going to see a clinic in Leeds that could help her. But when I went, they wouldn't speak to me."

"Can't you get access to their files through work?"

Charlie shook her head. "I don't work for the agency anymore. I haven't for two years."

Noah looked up sharply, deep eyes pinning her to the spot. "Why?"

She shook her head, not wanting to explain that she couldn't after what she'd done. Her guilt had almost crushed the life from her. "It doesn't matter. It does mean I don't have the resources anymore."

"And you want me to ask Shadow to help you?"

"I wouldn't ask if I wasn't desperate."

His sneer almost made her step back, but she had nowhere to go.

"Oh, I'm aware you want nothing to do with me. The divorce papers made that clear."

Biting her tongue to the point it almost bled she kept quiet. Nothing she could say would make it better, so why try.

Noah rubbed his hands over his face and cursed. "Fuck." He shoved his hands in his pockets and prowled closer, so close she could feel his heat through the black t-shirt he wore. The band of tattoos on his biceps flexed and she ached to touch him. "Fine, I'll speak to Bás and see if we can help. But I'm not making any promises."

The relief at his words felt like a weight lifted off her chest. "Thank you, Noah."

"Don't thank me, yet. He'll probably say no."

"I know but thank you for trying. It means a lot."

Noah nodded, a small movement of his head. "I'll call you."

"Thanks."

Just one word that would never be able to express how grateful she was.

CHAPTER 3

Bishop rapped his knuckles against Bás' partially open office door. "Knock, knock. You got a minute, boss?"

Bás looked up and motioned him in as he threw down the pen he'd been chewing on. "You saved me from expense reports, thank you."

Bishop smirked as he sank down onto the office chair and leaned back. He wasn't sure how he was going to do this or even why, but he'd promised her, and, unlike Charlie, he kept his promises. "Happy to help, just make sure an extra zero is added to my paycheck, and we'll call it even."

"Ha, you've got two hopes, Bob Hope and no hope."

Bishop chuckled. "Figures."

He wasn't really complaining, he got paid well. Better than he'd ever had been and more than that, Bás and the team had saved him. Without them, he had no doubt he would've eaten a bullet.

"What can I do for you? Because I know you didn't come in here to shoot the shit with me."

Bás watched him with intelligent eyes that missed nothing, his palms laid over the arms of the chair, relaxed, calm. Literally everything he wasn't feeling at this moment. "Charlie came to see me."

"Oh?"

"Her sister is missing. Andrea is younger than her, only twenty-one and she called a while back to say she was pregnant. Charlie says she sounded pretty upset. When Charlie got to her, she was gone. No sign of her, all her stuff had been packed by some unknown man with no forwarding address."

"I take it Charlie has looked for her?"

Bishop sat forward, his limbs tingling with excess energy. "Yeah, she can't find her. Apparently her Uni roommate mentioned a clinic she'd been talking about. Charlie went there but they won't discuss anything with her."

Bás picked up the pen he'd thrown down and twirled it in his fingers, his interest piqued despite his trying to hide it. Bishop had spent too long reading people and it was now so ingrained he didn't even have to try.

"She wants our help?"

"Yes, she isn't with MI5 anymore and doesn't have the resources."

"I'm aware."

Bishop looked up sharply. "You were?"

Bás sat forward, dropping the pen before resting his elbows on the desk. "Of course. Do you honestly think I would've allowed her help with Lucía if she hadn't been vetted by Watchdog first?"

Bishop shrugged. "I didn't think about it at all. I try not to let Charlie in my head, ever."

"So, you didn't keep up with her after you two parted ways?"

"Fuck, no. She made it clear she wasn't interested when she shot me and issued divorce papers. I have no idea what she's been up to since then."

"Hm."

"So, what do you think? Can we take this case? It might have a link to Project Cradle."

"It might, but then it could be as simple as she's run off with her boyfriend."

"True, but Andrea is a good kid. She went through a lot and their dad is a douchebag."

"It sounds like you want us to take this case."

Bishop blew out a breath through his lips and sat back, his hands flexing on the arms of the seat. "I guess I do."

"You guess? I need more than that, Bish. I won't fight for a case if the person bringing it to me isn't fully on board. What we do is dangerous, and if I ask those men and women out there to risk their lives I'm accountable for that. So, I need to be sure it's worthwhile."

"I know that, and I do want you to take it or put it to the team at least."

"Why?"

Bishop frowned. "Why?"

Bás stood and rounded the desk to come and lean against it next to where he was sitting. "Yes, why do you want to help the woman who shot you and then almost caused you to end your life?"

"I didn't."

Bás shook his head, holding up a hand. "Save it. I know you were moments away from taking your life some days. I've seen it and recognised it in you. You pulled yourself out of that dark place and every painful second of it was heavy with despair. Tell me why you want to risk going back there?"

Bishop had no idea that he'd been so transparent. He'd never told a soul how he was feeling. The first few weeks with Shadow had been the hardest but over time and with the help of his non-blood family, he'd allowed the scab to become a scar.

Looking up he eyed the man who was a mentor and friend and knew he deserved honesty. "We had a child, Charlie and me. A little boy. He was so perfect, with ten tiny fingers and toes, but there were complications and he was born too early at twenty-seven weeks. He only lived for twelve hours." His throat closed around the pain the memories brought. Nothing had prepared him for the love he'd felt, and nothing could ever have prepared him for the pain of losing him or watching Charlie mourn the loss. Her body was still healing while she tried to battle not only the hormones but her grief.

"I'm very sorry to hear that, Bishop."

Bishop nodded, not trusting himself to speak for a moment. "We called him Freddie." He blinked away the sudden dampness and stood, pushing away to pace the floor and get himself together before he responded to Bás' question. The truth was, he didn't know why he needed to help Charlie, just that when she'd asked, he felt an overprotective streak. A need to fix whatever was causing her pain and wasn't that fucked up? She was in the wrong and he wanted to fix things. "I can't turn my back on her, Bás. No matter what she's done, I can't let her do this alone if we can help."

"I understand. I'll put it to the team and see what they say."

Bishop closed his eyes relief washing over him.

"But if we do this, I won't have her going solo. My first priority is the team and always will be. You'll have to keep her in line and make sure she plays as a team member."

"I can do that."

Bás nodded as he folded his arms over his chest. "Good, then call everyone into the briefing room."

Bishop walked to the door but turned back. "Bás?"

His friend looked up from the piece of paper on his desk. "Yes?"

"Thank you and thanks for not giving up on me in the beginning. I know I was a mess."

"You had your reasons, and I could see your potential and I was right. I'm sorry you went through that."

"Me too. Can you keep it to yourself, please? I don't want to have to explain it."

Bás paused as if considering. "Yes of course, as long as it doesn't affect the mission if we take it. If that happens, I expect you to tell the team yourself. It's not lost on me that we're going into a case involving a pregnant woman. That's close to the knuckle for anyone, but I imagine doubly hard for you after what you've suffered."

"I'll be fine."

"I know that, but if you need any of us, we're here. That's how this team works."

"Agreed."

Bishop walked out of the room feeling like he'd been put through the emotional wringer and the evening wasn't over yet. The halls of the underground compound where the Shadow team lived and worked for the most part were brightly lit. The lights would dim around midnight allowing people to relax and retire to their apartments.

Each was designed to be what the occupant had instructed when the building was built. Some of the team, like Bein and Snow, and now Reaper, had property outside of the compound where they lived when they weren't on a case, but this was perfect for his needs. He had the privacy he needed without the loneliness he knew would cripple him.

Heading towards the sound of voices in the communal kitchen area where a lot of them ate, despite each apartment having a fully functioning kitchen, he saw Hurricane, Bein, Watchdog, and Titan talking with Duchess. For a second he wondered if Watchdog had told the others Charlie had been in the pub but dismissed it. Watchdog would never gossip like that, which was why his question earlier about Duchess had Bishop watching her closely now.

He hadn't expected to see her back when she'd arrived yesterday. She was working a really long case and had been for the best part of a year. He wasn't sure how she did it, but Duchess was a force to be reckoned with. As he looked more closely he could see the strain she carried in the tightness of her shoulders. Perhaps his friend was onto something.

"Bás wants us in the briefing room."

Bein clapped his hands together with glee. "We got a case?"

Bein was always lost when his fiancée was away in Birmingham studying nursing at Uni.

"Maybe. Are the others around?"

Duchess thumbed behind her at the apartments. "Val is in her apartment, Reaper is on his way back from Hereford still, but shouldn't be long. Snow is in the tech room doing something or other, and Lotus is talking to Rykov on the phone."

"We probably need them too." Nerves twisted his stomach at the thought of the focus being on him, even if it was through Charlie. He'd made no secret of what she'd done, being extremely vocal about his dislike of his ex-wife, but the truth was so much more complex than that.

He hated her for what she'd done. Not shooting him as much as the betrayal and the fact she'd thrown him away like he was nothing after all the promises they'd made to each other. She'd cheapened every single second they'd spent together, and that was what he couldn't forgive.

"I'll call them."

Bishop offered Duchess a grateful smile as he headed toward the briefing room and took his usual seat between Bein and Hurricane. Bás was already waiting at the head of the long table, his hands clasped in front of him. A stable, steady leader who they all looked up to, there was nobody better to lead Shadow. It might have been Jack who gave him this job, but it was Bás and his unflinching leadership and support that had made him the man he was today. A man who was about to face his past whether he wanted to or not.

His mind went back to Miss Rose and what she'd said to him tonight before he dismissed it as coincidence. That was all her warnings were, the ramblings of an old lady.

Val wandered in with her two shadows on her heels. Monty, the younger one was an Australian sheepdog. Scout, a German Shepherd, was a few years older and the more chill of the two. Both were exceedingly well trained. He'd be happy for either animal to have his back and yet they were still gentle with Fleur, Snow's niece and adopted daughter, which was weird but worked for her and Sebastian.

"Hey, Monty." The dog sniffed his hand, as he slumped beside his chair. Bishop buried his face in the dog's soft coat as Bás began.

"Bishop brought a case to me tonight that might have a lead to Project Cradle. At this point, the link is tenuous at best. It seems his ex-wife Charlie needs our help."

Bishop listened as Bás outlined the details as he'd given them, only speaking a few times to confirm a few details.

Bás looked around the room, his gaze stopping for the briefest second on Val before moving on. "We need to vote. As per the usual format, Bishop will sit this one out. I must stress that we have no concrete evidence that there's a link. At this point, it is purely conjecture."

Bás nodded and Bishop stood to leave the room. If there was a compromised party, they always left the room so anyone voting against the proposal would feel free to do so without judgement or repercussions. Nine times out of ten, the vote was discussed and anyone voting against had told the person why with no fallout.

He knew there was a very real chance the group would be against this. The link, like Bás had said, was weak and this was only personal for him because it was Charlie.

The thought made his lip curl in disgust at his own weakness. He wished he could hate her internally as much as he vocalised, it would make his life so much easier.

Pacing the hallway, his hands in the pockets of his jeans, it felt like a lifetime, but in reality, it was only a few minutes before Hurricane popped his head out.

"We're done." His grin made the knot in Bishop's belly loosen. The team had voted with him. Now he just had to work with Charlie without losing his mind.

CHAPTER 4

HER FOOT BOUNCED IN A NERVOUS RHYTHM SO UNLIKE HER THAT IT DREW Noah's attention from across the room. Stilling her foot, Charlie glanced toward the front where Bás speaking, hardly able to look at Noah without wanting him and not just because of the sexy way his t-shirt was stretched around his muscular frame.

When he'd called to say the team had decided to help, she'd felt giddy with relief. Her body almost sagged with the acknowledged exhaustion she was fighting. Since she'd gotten back from Prague, she'd only slept about six hours and that was four days ago. Those six hours had been filled with nightmares, leaving her groggier than before.

Glancing around the room, it was difficult to believe they were underground, but even with the cloth bag over her head, she'd been able to tell they were descending. Where abouts on the Welsh mountain they were though she had no clue. The set-up here was far sleeker and more elaborate than she'd ever imagined. It must have cost an absolute fortune, so the backer, whoever that was, had some serious money behind them.

Her mind drifted to her friend Jack, and she tried to picture him funding this. As far as she knew his brother Will was the one with more money than God, but perhaps she was wrong. Either way, Shadow had some serious funding. Not like the outfit she worked for which was basically a private investigator firm that was more ambulance chaser than anything else.

Not that she had that job now. She'd quit when they wouldn't give her time off to look for her sister. She didn't regret it, but it meant when she found her sister and finished this she'd need a new job. One thing was for sure, she wouldn't touch the money Noah put into her bank account every month as part of their divorce settlement.

She'd tried to refuse, but his lawyer had insisted he wouldn't sign the papers without her agreement, and she needed him to be free of her and what she'd done.

"Tell me again about your sister."

Duchess was leaning against the desk as she spoke with her arms folded and her ankles crossed as she watched her warily. The women here were fierce, and she'd already had a cool response from Lotus, who was the scariest of them all.

Charlie lifted her chin, steeling her spine. She was no slouch, and she couldn't allow these people who didn't know her to affect her. They had no idea why she'd done what she had, what had driven her, but a bigger part of her wanted to hug these people for having Noah's back. Nobody had done that for him before her, not truly. After she'd left, her biggest worry was that he'd blame himself and go off the deep end. Thank God he had these people to stabilise him and make sure he knew he was important.

"Yes, of course. Andrea is my half-sister. We share a father. She's studying Fashion Design at Manchester University and called me a few weeks back to say she was pregnant. She was very upset. I was on a job in Prague and promised to come and see her and help her figure it out when I got home. When I arrived, her roommate said she'd gone to some clinic and never came back. A man she didn't know had collected her things and she'd dropped out of Uni."

"Could she have gone off with the father?"

Charlie shrugged. "Honestly, I can't say for sure because I have no idea who the father is. Neither did the roommate, but I've looked for her everywhere. Every lead goes back to the clinic, and I still have no idea about the father of her child just that he's older than her and perhaps has money."

"Was she working?"

Charlie rested her jittery hands between her thighs. "Yes, at a bar."

"And they haven't seen her either?"

Hurricane was addressing her now, and she felt less hostility from him. He was a tall, black man, who was very muscular and handsome with a smile that transformed him from frightening to adorable. Not that she'd ever tell him that.

"No, she quit her job the same day she left Uni." Charlie wasn't sure whether she should add that her quitting had been the only good to come from this because the bar in question was known to be a strip club of dubious background.

"Name of the clinic?"

Watchdog leaned back on the two legs of his chair to speak to her, and Charlie wondered if it would collapse under his weight. He, too, was a big man, with solid strength and visible muscles under his Henley shirt. "Harmony Valley Medical. They're in Leeds but have a facility in London and Birmingham too."

Noah grimaced and the familiar gesture made her belly clench. "Urgh, could it be any more clichéd? Is there even a valley in Leeds?"

"When I went it was all very friendly and welcoming, with smiling staff and a painted airy reception, but I couldn't even get past the receptionist."

"Is it just a fertility clinic?"

Charlie went to answer Hurricane's question but Watchdog beat her to it.

"They're a fertility clinic and offer other Gynaecological services, such as terminations, sterilisations, etcetera, but they also facilitate adoptions. They're owned by an American company, but I suspect that's a shell company. Give me a few minutes and I'll have a name for you."

"Any dirt on them?"

Noah moved up behind Watchdog, who was typing at the speed of light on a laptop on the conference room table. Charlie moved closer, wanting to see what he found, which she knew was an excuse to be close to Noah.

"Not a single thing, which itself is suspicious. All big medical companies attract complaints of some degree but there's nothing but glowing references on the web. I'll need to go darker."

"Doesn't mean they go around kidnapping young girls or stealing their babies though."

Watchdog arched an eyebrow at Val, who by far seemed the most approachable of the group. "No, but when you project an image of perfection, it's usually to hide some pretty big flaws."

"True, so what's your excuse, Watchdog? Flaws and secrets?" Titan clapped his friend on the back and laughed.

"Fuck you, I'm perfection."

"Yeah of course you are, Mr Walking Encyclopaedia."

"I can't help it if I have brains and beauty."

"And a vision problem too, my friend." Lotus jumped up to sit on the desk as she joined in the playful banter.

"Focus, children. Honestly, it's like running a fucking day care around here."

Bás' deep voice was short but when Charlie glanced at him it was to see him hiding a smirk. This team were more than friends, they were family, and she was so glad that Noah had that in his life. He'd lost too much in his lifetime, starting when he was just a few days old, and she hoped ending when she'd walked away leaving him bleeding.

"Okay, this may take a bit longer than I thought. They have some pretty impressive firewalls for a medical company."

"We should go in. A snapshot of the files will only show us so much. I want to take a look around. If this is related to Cradle we need to know, now."

Charlie looked at Duchess and agreed with her. "I agree."

"Undercover?" Noah pushed his hands into his back pockets, drawing her eyes to his tight ass in his jeans. That had always been her favourite look on him, relaxed sexy as hell.

"I think it's our best bet to start with. Go in as a couple wanting fertility treatment and ask about the clinic. We can have a back story of failed attempts or even suggest we've been let down in the past, so they work for the business."

"That will work to get us through the door for sure, not sure what it will show us."

"It might be they have paper files we can access."

"Either way, it's worth a shot," Bás concluded.

"I want to go in and look around. If I see my sister, she's more likely to come with me than you."

"I doubt very much they'd keep her there if they've kidnapped her."

"True, but on the off chance."

Bás shrugged. "Fine, Hurricane can go with you as your husband."

"No!"

Charlie's head shot up to look at Noah, who was gritting his jaw.

"Let me go. With our history, we're more likely to pull off the intimacy of a married couple."

Duchess eyed him and then her. "You sure about this, Bish?"

Noah dipped his head. "Yes. We can fake it for a small time. Just don't give her a gun and I should be fine."

His joke made the team laugh, but for Charlie, her gut twisted with defeat. He'd never forgive her, and she had to stop hoping for a miracle. Getting her sister back was her priority now and should always be. Noah forgiving her was a lost cause.

His eyes moved over her as if he could sense every thought in her head. His lips pursed as if he was about to say something, but he looked away with a frown instead.

"Okay. Watchdog, get me backgrounds in the digital universe for these two. Work up a background with a few fertility companies and job histories etcetera. In a few days Duchess, Hurricane, Bishop, and Charlie will head to Leeds. Lotus and Bein, you check out the Birmingham site, and Val and I will check London. Snow and Reaper will stay here with Titan and help Watchdog work through any links to Cradle. If it's there, find it. I think this is the tip of the iceberg and we can't have this continue."

CHAPTER 5

HAVING CHARLIE IN HIS SPACE FELT WEIRD, BUT RIGHT IN A WAY THAT MADE him angry. Her hand brushed over the fabric of his couch as she walked around his living space. The apartment had light laminate wood flooring in a pale oak, pale green paint on the walls in the main living area, and white cabinets in the open-plan kitchen. The cream couch faced a glass coffee table and a fifty-two-inch tv that he rarely watched.

"This place is lovely."

"Thanks."

The awkwardness he felt was strange, but he didn't know how to act. He knew how his body was reacting, he wanted her, he always had. From the first day they'd met she'd had an allure that he'd never been able to resist. Now, though, it warred with a deep wariness of her, along with an anger and bitterness that overrode his feelings of desire—almost.

Charlie was tall, nearly five feet eight in her bare feet, slim, but with a round ass that drove him wild, and breasts that made his mouth water. Rosey-skinned with long honey-blonde hair, she was like his perfect woman wrapped in a delicious package and she'd never seemed aware of just how beautiful she was. Her blue eyes had a hint of green when she was aroused, so expressive and alive, watched him now with the same wariness he felt.

"This is awkward, right?"

Noah laughed. Trust Charlie to cut straight to the heart of the matter. "Yeah, I guess more than I thought it would be."

She walked toward him, and it took everything in him not to sweep her into his arms as he'd done so many times before and kiss the little scar at the back of her ear which made her shiver.

"Tell me about the team. They seem to be a close bunch."

Noah relaxed, his friends were a safe topic. Moving to sit on the couch, he watched her take the opposite end, turning towards him and twisting her leg beneath her as she leaned against the arm of the couch.

"What do you want to know?"

Charlie tucked her hands in her sleeves, something she'd always done when she was nervous and the feeling made him want to fix it for her as he'd always done, but she wasn't his to protect now.

"I want to know what you can tell me."

"Well, Bein is solid. He's Scottish Royalty and I mean that in a literal sense. He's getting married to Aoife next year and she's training to be a nurse. Snow is a former jewel thief and married to a judge and they have Fleur, who's their niece and they're raising."

"Wow, a jewel thief and a judge. That's like a romance movie."

"Yeah, it started more like a thriller but they got there in the end and are so ridiculously happy it's vomit inducing." He smiled thinking of them and the future they had before them, even as the envy that he no longer had it stirred under his rib cage. "You know Reaper's story as you were there for that."

"I still can't believe he got himself a Princess."

"He deserves it. He's one of the best men I know."

"Oh, I wasn't suggesting otherwise."

Noah stood, feeling antsy again. The setting, similar to so many of their Friday nights, was making him forget what she'd done, and he couldn't allow himself to soften towards her. "Have you eaten?"

Charlie shook her head and he wondered how she managed to stay alive. She was shit at looking after herself. She was great at looking after other people, but she always put herself last. "I can make you some eggs and bacon. You still like Tabasco on your eggs?"

Standing, she followed him to the kitchen and leaned against the island. "I certainly do."

A memory of her running to the bathroom sick after he'd made her eggs and later finding out she was pregnant with Freddie flashed in his mind's eye, making him pause as he looked in the fridge. Taking a second to pretend he was looking for something he got himself together and turned back to the hob with a blank look on his face, only to see her blinking as if she too was fighting tears.

Noah wanted to ignore it, to run from the pain that was crushing for them both, pain that had driven a wedge between them he hadn't seen coming until it was too late.

Clearing his throat, he set about whisking the eggs as Charlie got herself together, giving her privacy to do so when all he wanted to do was take her in his arms and hold her and tell her he felt it too. That it would be okay and they'd get through this, but they hadn't.

Placing the bacon under the grill, he let it begin to cook, and popped two slices of toast in the toaster while he gently stirred the eggs. Once it was all done, he plated up and added a generous splash of tabasco for Charlie. He personally liked his taste buds and had no intention of burning them off with that red poison.

Charlie tucked in and moaned, sending a shot of lust straight to his dick, so many images of her making that same sound while she had her lips around his dick making him groan and cough to hide the response.

"Still hate tabasco I see."

Noah glanced at his plate still lost in lustful thoughts and struggled to catch up. "Oh, yeah. Horrible disgusting stuff."

Charlie's laugh was like a dose of sunshine, warm and sweet. She was as deadly as anyone on this team, fiercer in hand-to-hand combat than he would ever be, but she still retained her sweetness. Or at least she had until one day he'd woken up and that sweetness was shrouded with grey resentment.

They ate in silence then, some of the awkwardness gone as the sounds of someone else in his apartment gave him a feeling of comfort. He hated being alone, he'd spent most of his life losing people, first his parents to an accident when he was three months old and then his adoptive parents when he was nineteen. He should be used to it, but he hated any time he could allow his emotions to sweep into that free space and eat him up.

"That was delicious."

Noah took her empty plate and moved to the sink to soak it in water.

"You must have been hungry."

"Starving, I haven't eaten in ...." She looked up to the ceiling as if thinking and shrugged. "It doesn't matter."

"Still the same old Charlie, not looking after yourself."

She waved him away as she'd always done. "I'm fine."

"Of course you are. I bet you haven't slept in days either."

Her hand came up to the dark circles under her eyes and he clenched his back teeth to keep from lecturing her about it.

"You know I don't sleep well."

Noah moved closer, his hand lifting without thinking about it as he swept a thumb over the evidence of her lack of self-care. Charlie's breath hitched in her chest, and she stilled as if too afraid to take a breath and break the spell. He didn't know what he was doing or why, but he revelled in the feel of her soft skin beneath his fingers. "You need to take better care of yourself."

"Why do you care?"

That was the million-dollar question, wasn't it? Why couldn't he stop himself from wanting to protect her? Why couldn't he hate her in a way that made it so much easier to keep her away? "I don't know."

His honesty had her lifting herself on her toes and bringing her lips close to his. He only had to lean in and he'd be able to lose himself in her as he'd done a hundred times. To feel the chemistry that was clearly still as strong as ever between them.

He stepped back, putting space between them as he ran his hand through his hair, turning his back on her. "We should talk about the visit to the clinic, get our stories straight."

He heard her clear her throat and when she spoke there was no trace of the lust from just seconds ago.

"Yes, of course."

Noah took a seat at the island and Charlie leaned against the back of the couch and they were back to awkward again. "What story are we going with?"

Charlie bit her bottom lip, her eyes to the ceiling buying time as she considered things. "How about we're a working couple with decent jobs so they don't question the fact we can afford multiple failed IVF attempts. Tell them we have no reason but unexplained infertility and two failed egg transfers."

Bishop blinked wondering how she knew so much about this but didn't voice his question. That might lead to a more intimate conversation, and he wasn't up for that tonight. Not when he was barely hanging on by a thread as it was. "That will work. Watchdog can work up a background based on that."

Charlie brushed her hand over the couch back again, a new nervous habit she'd not had before.

"Will you be okay doing this?"

Her blue eyes pierced him with a stare, a challenge in it that he had no intention of accepting. "Yes, of course, it's just acting, right?"

Charlie swallowed and he wondered if she was going to bring up the shooting and the past so filled with pain it was like walking among landmines.

He needed her out of there so he could foster that uncaring façade back into place. "I have a few things to do. Would you like me to walk you to your rooms?"

Charlie shook her head. "No, I can manage."

She angled her body toward the door, and he followed, opening it for her and watching her step through. He could feel the hurt he'd caused by his abrupt eviction of her from his apartment and hated that he cared.

"Night, Noah."

"Goodnight, Charlie. Try and get some sleep. We'll find Andrea."

Her tight smile was all he got in response. Closing the door, he leaned against it and sighed. This might be his toughest case yet.

CHAPTER 6

CHARLIE WOKE FEELING GROGGY, THE FEW HOURS OF SLEEP SHE'D MANAGED had been plagued with dreams of loss and death. Tossing back the covers, she swung her bare legs over the side and stood. She needed coffee, preferably in an IV in her arm but a cup would do to start. Moving through the apartment she noticed the differences between this one and Noah's place. This had white walls and cool grey flooring. Heated from below, it was warm and everything was new and clean, but it was impersonal. Noah's home was decorated in warm tones, similar to what they'd had in their house when they were married.

Pressing the start button on the coffee machine, she headed for the shower. She had a job to do and that didn't include comparing home décor. Throwing her hair into a bun, she showered quickly and efficiently, not giving herself time to think. It was so different from how she'd been, but now she knew if she thought too much the weight of the pain from everything would crush her soul.

Dressing in her soft, blue skinny jeans, a white t-shirt, and a green bomber jacket, she slipped her feet into black biker boots. Using make-up to cover the dark circles, she recalled the feel of

Noah's fingers on her skin. He'd seen through her disguise, past the make-up and confidence. He'd always seen her, it was one of the things she loved about him. Except now she didn't want him seeing her weakness. Calling her out for not looking after herself had been typical Noah. He cared about everyone and if she allowed herself to think it was anything else, she was in for a serious amount of heartbreak.

Pouring black coffee into a travel cup, she added two large sugars and headed out to find someone to talk to. She just couldn't stay here and wallow in pity and what-ifs.

The corridors were quiet, but it was still early at barely seven am. The doors to the apartments were sound proofed which was a bonus for these people who had to live here and required privacy.

Light from under the door of the tech room had her pausing, not sure of her welcome. Deciding she'd just go in and ask for an update on the case, she knocked on the door and followed the muffled command to enter.

Watchdog had his back to her with his feet up on the desk as he tossed a ball in the air and caught it, but turned when she came in.

"Sorry to disturb you. I just wondered if there was an update."

Dropping his feet to the floor, he offered her a smile and a nod. "Come take a seat and I'll show you what I've found."

Charlie could sense some of the answers she sought in his voice and pulled up the rolling chair beside him. "What did you find?"

He clicked a few buttons on his keyboard and on the giant screen to her left she saw an image of Andrea.

A gasp shot out of her mouth as she watched her sister walk into the fertility clinic she'd been to asking questions. There was no audio, but she spoke with the receptionist and almost immediately a man came through the locked double doors leading to the main part of the clinic and led her away. She didn't recognise the man, and his demeanour was curt and clinical. Andrea, for her part, looked nervous but not frightened in any way or like she was being forced.

Charlie glanced at Watchdog as the clip ended. "Is there any more?"

"No, but as far as I can find, she never exits the clinic. At least not from this way and if she left through another door, it's been erased from the CCTV."

Charlie dropped her head to the mug still clutched in her hand. "Damn it."

"You showed her?"

Her head spun to the door to see Noah walking toward them looking annoyed. He stopped a few feet short of her and looked at Watchdog.

"She has the right to know, and the rest of the team knows."

"What?"

Charlie felt anger pummel her chest that she was the last to know such a significant development. Her gaze swung to Noah who looked a little sheepishly at the ground before lifting his eyes to her.

His gaze was steel as he silently challenged her. "You were exhausted, and I thought you needed the rest. It was my call."

Hurt and anger and a multitude of other emotions she couldn't even begin to unravel wound through her, but she concentrated on the anger. Anger was safe in this new, confusing world. "No, Noah, it wasn't your call." She stalked forward, placing her coffee on the side console as her fists clenched at her sides. She pointed at the screen behind her, her hand almost shaking now. "That's my sister, and I should've been woken as soon as Watchdog found this."

Noah pushed his hands into his pockets and smirked at her. "Are you fucking kidding me? You could hardly stand from exhaustion last night."

Charlie got up in his face now, so close she could see the tick in his eye which was a tell of his real feelings. Chest heaving, she tried to control her emotions, knowing that around this man she never behaved how she thought she should. His eyes dropped to her chest and the angry tick turned his eyes dark with lust. Heat bloomed between her legs as his breathing became choppier.

"I'm not your problem, Noah."

"The fuck you're not. You're my wife."

"Ex-wife."

He stilled at her correction before ignoring the comment entirely. "I apologise for being a decent human being and considering your health, Charlie. I won't make that mistake again." With that he spun on his heel, heading for the door. "Food is ready in the kitchen."

Watchdog jumped to his feet and ran after Noah like his ass was on fire and she hated that he'd witnessed the animosity between them. No, she hated that it existed in the first place and that she'd been the one to ruin them.

Dropping her head into her hands, she swore at her own stupidity. Noah was doing her a favour, and even after everything she'd done, he still cared enough to want her to be fully rested. But if she allowed him those liberties it was only a matter of time before she allowed hope into her heart. With every kind thing he did, her dumb heart wanted to argue that maybe there was a way back, but her brain knew there was no happy ever after for them. Too much damage had been done, the rot had set in long before the shooting. No, the beginning of their end was the night their son died in his daddy's arms.

Needing to get away from her own thoughts, she ran out of the door and headed for the loud sounds of talking and laughter. Finding the entire team in the kitchen filling plates with food, she felt lost. This was a group of friends and she'd never felt more alone than she did right then.

"Hey, grab a plate. This lot will go back for seconds before the rest of us get a chance." Valentina motioned for the plates and Charlie smiled gratefully. The scent of bacon, maple syrup, toast, and coffee filled the space as she walked up to a huge buffet of food.

"Wow, this is a lot of food."

Valentina smirked. "Yeah because these guys think eating is an Olympic sport."

Charlie followed the line of her thumb to the table where the others were all laughing and eating like one big happy messy family. Noah looked up at that second pinning her with his gaze.

There were so many emotions between them that she had to look away from the intensity in his eyes. "I guess this is a pretty physical job."

"It can be, and we train hard but we always try and eat breakfast together when we're all here, which isn't as often as we'd like."

Placing bacon, toast, and a waffle on her plate, she followed Val to the huge coffee and tea pots. "You're like family."

Valentina cocked her head and smiled. "Not like family, we are family. Just not by blood."

A knot of envy and loss tightened in her belly as she glanced at the group. "That's nice."

"Yeah, it is, and necessary. You can't fight for each other like we do if you're not committed."

"Not fighting doesn't mean you aren't committed."

Valentina put a hand on her arm to get her attention. "I didn't mean anything by it. I don't know your story, but I know that whatever you did, you had your reasons."

"You do?"

"Of course. You'd need to be blind not to see the connection you two have."

Charlie blushed but ignored the heat from her cheeks as she took a seat at the end of the table beside Val and opposite Hurricane. The long table put Noah down on the other end, and she was grateful for the space. "I think you may have misinterpreted that look of hatred from Noah."

Valentina shoved a dainty piece of bacon in her mouth and chewed as she shook her head. "Uh-uh. Chemistry I tell you. You're not done yet. I can feel it."

"Oh, God, not you too, Val. You're as bad a Miss Rose."

Val pointed her fork at Hurricane. "You mark my words, Hurricane."

"Who is Miss Rose?" Charlie was feeling more and more confused by the second.

Hurricane pushed his empty plate away and leaned on the table, his grin infectious. "Miss Rose is Mrs Jones' ninety-five-year-old mother and a self-confessed physic. She only got to the village last night and has already issued cryptic advice to both Bishop and Duchess."

"Sounds like a load of old rubbish to me."

"I agree."

Charlie almost bit her tongue trying not to ask what she'd said to Noah. Hurricane's smirk told he knew it too.

"Well, you two cynics can believe what you like. Personally, I'm going to be rooting for the home team."

Val had finished her breakfast as Charlie picked at hers, her appetite not what it was. "The home team?"

"You and Bish. I don't know what happened, but my bet is it's fixable."

Charlie sighed deeply and pushed her plate away, the last of her desire for food now gone. She wished Valentina was right, but she knew better.

Glancing at Noah, she found him watching her over the top of his coffee mug. He was so handsome, not just outwardly but he was beautiful inside too and she'd broken him. "Some things can't be fixed."

Val squeezed her arm in comfort, and she blinked away the tears she felt building. She was more broken than ever, and she had nobody to blame but herself.

"Want to help me with some training with Scout and Monty?"

Charlie nodded and stood. "Sounds good, but no more matchmaking ideas. Noah and I are done. Like a Taylor Swift song."

She gave Hurricane a small smile at his chuckle and turned to go with Valentina. Some time away from Noah would help her get her equilibrium back on track hopefully.

CHAPTER 7

"Take it easy, Bish." Hurricane blocked the kick Bishop sent his way and countered with a low jab.

"Can't handle a little sparring, Hurricane?"

"I can handle whatever you dish out, but I don't want to have to hurt you and embarrass you in front of our audience."

Bishop turned to see who he was talking about and got caught by a sweep to the ankle. His body landed hard on the matt; the wind knocked out of him as Hurricane's grinning face appeared over him. "Asshole move."

"Maybe but I needed to do something to slow you down. You're like a fucking machine today. Anything you want to talk about?"

Hurricane offered his hand and Bishop waved it away, jumping to his feet and unwrapping his hands from the tape. "Nah, nothing."

"You sure it's good her being here, man?"

Bishop knew exactly who his friend was talking about. Charlie was everywhere, laughing and chatting with all his friends, but with him, there was just a cold shield of ice. "It's not forever and we have a plan now. We're heading out later this morning."

It was only seven am and he'd needed to get a workout in if he was going to survive this undercover happily ever after with his ex-wife.

"True, but if you need to talk, I'm here. Okay?"

Hurricane was a good guy, one of the best and from all accounts, one of the best pilots the Royal Air Force had ever seen. Bishop didn't know his story as he kept it to himself. Only Bás and Duchess were privy to that, but whatever it was, they were lucky to have him.

Bishop slapped his friend's shoulder. "Thank you, man."

Walking back to the changing rooms, he and Hurricane went over the plan again. He and Duchess would be back-up for him and Charlie as they went into the clinic. Bishop couldn't say he wasn't concerned about it, being involved in anything to do with kids was hard for him but it would be doubly hard for Charlie. While she clearly hated him, he'd come to the realisation he couldn't hate her.

Showered and changed, he headed toward Bás' office and found the door open with Charlie sitting opposite his boss.

Surprise and wariness snaked down his spine at seeing her there.

Bás waved him inside. "Bishop, come in."

Charlie looked at him from under long eyelashes and glanced away. She was still avoiding him. *Great!*

"Charlie was just telling me how she knew Jack Granger back in the day."

Bishop's gaze flew to his ex-wife in shock. "You did?"

Her small nod and the fact she couldn't seem to look him in the eye made him suspicious. She was hiding something. "How?"

"We worked a couple of cases together when you were in Iraq on assignment."

Bishop sat in the seat beside her, remembering the time she was talking about. It wasn't long after they'd met, and they worked cases independently. He'd been stationed in the fucking sandbox for six months as the usual case officer had been injured and he spoke fluent Arabic. "You never mentioned it."

Charlie shrugged. "It didn't seem important."

"Hmm."

Bishop tightened his grip on the arm of the chair as he processed the knowledge. Charlie knew the man who'd rescued him and subsequently offered him his place here in Shadow. Coincidence? He didn't think so.

"Are you two all set for today?"

Charlie nodded at Bás. "Yes. I believe so."

"Actually, there are a few things if you have time, Charlie."

She looked wary. "Oh, okay."

Bás stood. "Perhaps you two can drive up together and discuss it. I don't want us to get caught in traffic and end up late."

"Yeah, sure, that works."

Perhaps a few hours in the car would help him figure this link out.

An hour later they were on the road with him in the driver's seat and Charlie holding on to the seat as her inner control freak tried to find peace.

"Still hate being a passenger, I see."

Charlie physically relaxed her death grip on the seat. "Some things don't change."

"And others do."

"Yeah, I guess."

Concentrating as he changed lanes and merged onto the motorway, Bishop thought about how best to ask the question mulling around his brain, without causing a fight.

"Ask what you need to ask, Noah."

He glanced at her to see her eyes still on the scenery outside. "Did you ask Jack to give me this job?"

"No. I arranged for him to be there to extract you after I shot you, but I didn't ask him to give you this job, I had no idea he was involved in Shadow until now." Her eyes came to him then and he had to look away from the warmth in them. "That was all you, Noah. You made a name for yourself at the agency, and he clearly needed someone with your skills on his team."

49

"So you planned to leave way before that night at Armand's villa?"

"I wanted my bases covered."

"That's not a fucking answer, Charlie."

She threw up her hands, twisting in her seat to face him. "What do you want from me, Noah?"

"The truth."

"You know the truth. I fucked up. I wrecked our world, and I gave you an out."

"An out?" His heart rate was spiking along with his blood pressure. "I never wanted an out, Charlie. I loved you."

"And you hated me."

Bishop frowned and shook his head in confusion. "What? No."

"You may not have said it, but each day we tore more pain from each other. I couldn't even look at you some days without seeing—"

She stopped suddenly on a choked cry and slapped her hand over her mouth. The cabin of the car was filled with emotion and pain as he allowed her to get herself together. He knew what she was going to say, and the guilt almost swallowed him whole. "Without seeing Freddie."

Charlie shook her head. "I can't do this now, Noah. Please."

Her voice was a dry husk as she pleaded with him, and he couldn't deny her anything. Not then and certainly not now. "Fine."

Bishop turned on the radio, finding a station he knew she loved and felt his heart kick in his chest when she gave him a grateful tilt of her lips. Perhaps now wasn't the time for this conversation. They needed to get in the right head space for these next few hours and talking about the loss they'd shared wasn't it.

"Do you have the bugs Watchdog gave you?"

She checked her bag at her feet. "Yes. Are they military grade?"

"Yes, we get lots of new tech from Will Granger to try out. He's constantly testing new designs."

"Is he the money behind Shadow then?"

Bishop pursed his lips and shrugged. "Honestly, I have no idea.

I've never really thought about it. The deep stuff was always your domain. I'm the brawn, you were the beauty and brains."

"Don't do that, Noah. You were the brains too. We were a good team."

She seemed to realise she'd gone too deep because she looked away and the car felt too small to contain them both.

"Actually, I think Watchdog is the brains."

Charlie looked at him. "Oh my God, right? Does he know a fact about everything on the planet?"

"I had no idea the world contained eight-point-seven-billion species and that every day around one hundred and fifty go extinct."

"It's crazy how smart he is. Although some facts I wish he'd keep to himself."

"Yeah, I can imagine."

Her chuckle stirred something inside him, and he wished more than anything in the world his clever friend knew how to turn back time.

CHAPTER 8

"Are you sure they won't recognise you?"

Since arriving in Leeds around lunchtime, Charlie had felt the change in Noah. In the last few days, she'd seen, angry, sexy, amused, annoyed, and now his face was etched with worry. "Seriously, when did you become such an old woman?"

"When I started my knitting club."

Laughter burst from her lips at his proclamation and she glanced across the car at him. He looked refreshed after a shower and change before they'd headed out. His natural metabolism seemed to tolerate less rest than she typically needed. Probably why he looked as drop-dead gorgeous as ever and she was barely pulling off homeless wreck. His smile as he looked at her made his eyes crinkle and she fought the urge to lift her hand and stroke his cheek.

This, the easiness between them was what she missed the most. When Bás had thrown her under the bus about knowing Jack she'd expected fall out, but Noah had taken her at her word which was more than she knew she would've done. The tenseness between them caused by the fight in the tech room that first morning had eased. Mainly because Noah had avoided her, and she'd calmed down and seen the gesture for what it had been. Her ex-husband was a good man and cruelty had never been his style.

His eyes moved back to the road as he drove toward the clinic, where her sister had gone for help.

"So apart from knitting, what else do you do for fun?"

She was glad they were alone in the car, and the comms switched off until they got to the location. It allowed her time with him that she'd otherwise not get and she wanted that more than anything. No matter how hard it was for her broken heart.

"I read, I work out, I train with the team, drink beer in the pub, but honestly, we don't get a lot of down time."

"Do you enjoy it?"

She watched his muscles bunch as he navigated the roundabout. "I do. We make a difference, one target at a time. No red tape, no political bullshit to wade through like a freaking landmine."

"I'm glad." And she was. At least he had that to cling to and good friends by the looks and sounds of it.

"What about you?"

Charlie blew out a breath. "Well, I'm currently jobless, since my employer fired me for leaving to help my sister."

"What an asshole."

"Yeah, he was but I was going to leave anyway."

"Can't settle?"

His knowing look made her drop her gaze from his keen eyes. "You know me. I never got into this work because I wanted to be a spy. I was just good at it, and it was a way out for me."

"You could retrain. You're only thirty-one. Plenty of time to figure it out and change paths."

"That would require me to know what I want to do instead."

Noah pulled into the carpark of the facility and cut the engine and turned to her. "You could be anything you want, Charl."

She couldn't admit to him that the only role she'd ever wanted was to be his wife and she'd blown it. "We should head in. Our appointment is in five minutes."

Noah looked like he was going to say something but just jerked his head in agreement. "Let's do this."

Lifting her hand, she switched on the comms and did a quick sound check with Watchdog, who was overseeing from base, and Duchess and Hurricane, who were their back-up in case things went sideways. Not that she thought it would. This was an initial assessment to get the vibe of the place.

Having so much backup was unusual for her, but she found she liked it. Or perhaps it was having her partner back by her side that felt so right.

Noah exited the car and came around the passenger side to meet her, his hand sliding into hers as naturally as if they'd done this just yesterday. His strong grip grounded her in a way that she hadn't felt since before they'd lost Freddie. She'd worn wide-leg trousers in black and a short-sleeved cream blouse with puff sleeves.

Her cover was that she was a professional in marketing and made good bank. Noah was in a short-sleeved polo shirt with dark-wash jeans. His cover was that he was a gym instructor. If the facility checked, they'd find a five-year marriage, multiple failed IVF attempts, and a decent savings account. With her wages in the six-figure category, it would explain away why IVF hadn't depleted those savings.

Charlie let her eyes wander around looking for cameras and spotting more than she thought were necessary for the place. The thought of Andrea here filled her stomach with a pit of ice.

"You okay?"

Noah's lips brushed her ear, and she felt the goosebumps grace her skin from the simple touch. "I was just thinking about Andrea and how scared she might be."

Stopping them, Noah turned toward her, placing his hands on her hips he pulled her close, looking for all the world like a husband reassuring his wife. The weight of the wedding and engagement ring on her finger felt right, but not as right as seeing the matching one on Noah's left hand.

"We're going to get her back. I promise you that, Charlie, and this time I won't let you down."

She had no time to respond as he kissed her temple and taking her hand, pulled her toward the front door, which swooshed open automatically.

Switching into operator mode was harder than she thought after that, but she focused on the chirpy receptionist, who was different from the last one she'd seen.

"Mr and Mrs Salisbury to see Dr Joseph."

Noah's voice was clear and strong as he spoke, allowing her to get her shit together.

Miss Chirpy batted her eyelashes at him, but just like when they were actually married, he didn't seem to notice.

"If you'd like to take a seat and fill out these forms, I'll let Dr Joseph know you're here."

"Thank you."

Charlie snatched the papers from the woman's hand, her jealousy spilling over slightly and causing a raised brow from Noah. Why were men so oblivious when women flirted with them?

Noah guided her to a seat with his hand on her back and she fought the irrational desire to swat it away.

Leaning in, he whispered in her hair. "What's wrong?"

Ignoring the form on a clipboard on her lap, she pulled back to look at his gorgeous tawny eyes. "Nothing. I just think it would be better for this mission if you didn't flirt with the receptionist."

A deep chuckle reverberated up his throat. "Well, this is new. You were never the jealous type before."

"I'm not jealous, asshat," she hissed between her teeth.

Noah grinned and planted a kiss square on her lips. "Course you're not."

Her reply was cut short as a doctor in black wingtips and pressed grey trousers interrupted them.

"Mr and Mrs Salisbury, I'm Dr Joseph. It's a pleasure to meet you."

Dr Joseph was medium height, with dark hair, greying at the temples and dark, ebony skin. His glasses perched on the tip of his nose and his smile was warm and genuine. Despite the reason for being there, Charlie found herself wanting to trust him. He wasn't the man she'd seen on the screen leading Andrea away and that was good. Although Watchdog was running facial on him and doing a search.

"Thank you for seeing us on short notice."

"My pleasure. Shall we?" He ushered them down a well-lit corridor the pale grey of the walls covered in brightly coloured obscure artwork with little titled placards below each piece. His office was large with an exam table along the right-side wall, cabinets beneath the window, and a wooden desk. One wall of the room was filled with images of cherubic little faces.

Pulled like a magnet Charlie moved across to get a closer look and take in all the babies in the pictures, some with hair and some completely bald. Some with scrunched-up faces and others looking beatific. All of them were a miracle of nature. Her gut rolled and clenched, and she let it come knowing it would help her cover to let this man see her pain.

"My success stories. I always ask for a picture for my wall to show my patients when they walk in that there's always hope."

"That's beautiful."

Dr Joseph clasped his hands in front of him. "I agree."

Her gaze moved to Noah who was watching her, his expression belying the pain she knew he was feeling. The loss of their own child was an open wound that would never heal.

"We shall begin with a history and then an exam and go from there."

Charlie took her seat next to Noah, allowing him to reach over and clasp her hand, threading their fingers and holding them on his lap. The next fifteen minutes were spent giving Dr Joseph the story they'd rehearsed.

"Have you ever carried a pregnancy to any kind of term?"

The question caught her off guard and Charlie tried to swallow the bile speeding up her throat. Sweat dotted her brow and she blinked to clear the tears.

"We lost a child at twenty-seven weeks."

Her gaze swung to Noah at the admission which was off-script and his hand tightened on hers, but he didn't look at her.

"I'm sorry. Do you know what the cause was? I have nothing in your records."

"We were living abroad at the time," Noah quickly added.

"I see."

"I fell."

Noah's eyes moved over her face as she looked at him. Anguish and guilt cut her insides like sharp blades as Charlie placed a hand over her flat stomach. She'd loved being pregnant, the feel of her son kicking and turning. Lying with Noah with his hand over her belly as he sang the wrong lyrics to their favourite song to their baby.

"I'd climbed on a chair to reach something and fell. It put me into early labour, but he was too little and didn't survive."

"It was my fault." Noah's voice was like gravel as he whispered his admission.

"What? No. I knew better than to climb. I was impatient and stupid. I should've waited."

"And I should have built the crib so you didn't feel you had to."

Emotion was thick in the room as they bared their souls in front of a man who'd probably seen this a thousand times.

"If I may?"

Charlie blinked and turned to the doctor, forcing her eyes away from the open wound of the man she loved.

"I think you both have a lot of built-up and misplaced guilt over this loss. A loss that was most likely nothing to do with the fall."

"The doctor said it was."

Dr Joseph looked at them over his glasses. "Well, without the file I can't say for sure, but I do know some counselling would be good for you both. There's a lot of guilt here and IVF is brutal."

Charlie didn't want to go down that path, she already felt like her soul had been ripped open for all to see. "Is it possible to see the facilities?"

"Yes, of course. Let me show you around."

Charlie felt air expand in her lungs as the doctor gave her a brief reprieve from the depth of emotion in the room.

He led them through wide double doors, away from the exam rooms using a lanyard on his hip to unlock the door. Back here things were more sterile and less opulent. People wore scrubs and comfy shoes, and men and women in lab coats chatted in the hallways. It was busy and she couldn't help thinking at least part of this operation was above the table and genuine.

"This is very much like a hospital," Charlie stated as Noah walked beside her, his hand once again entangled with hers.

"Yes, we have exam rooms at the front and then our labour and delivery wards back here. There's also a ward for our mothers who are staying long term because of complications."

"Do those arise a lot?"

"No, usually it's multiples that cause the mother to need bed rest or if they have a medical morbidity that makes the pregnancy more complex."

"You perform other services like terminations here?"

Noah's question made the doctor stop short. "We do, Mr Salisbury. Every woman has the right to decide what happens to her body and we offer that to them here. We also facilitate adoptions for those that feel they cannot terminate but aren't able to raise the child themselves."

"Do you see a lot of that?"

"More than I'd like to, I'm afraid."

"You don't approve?"

"No, on the contrary, I believe in freedom of choice. But it saddens me that an unwanted pregnancy happens as much as it does. It's never easy for mothers to give a child away or end a pregnancy. Ah, here we are, here's the nursery."

Dr Joseph stopped at a window and Charlie braced herself to look at the tiny faces. Five small clear plastic bassinets were in the middle of the room. Five identical faces stared back at her. Tiny bodies wrapped in white blankets, little pink or blue hats on their heads. Arms came around her waist and she leaned back into Noah's strength as an ache deep inside her threatened to overwhelm her. His entire body wrapped her up and held her together, his lips on her hair, his heart pounding as hard as hers was.

"This was a difficult pregnancy, but mum and babies are doing well. All six will go home soon and then the fun really begins."

"They're perfect."

"Yes they are, and we'll get that for you, too. Your files suggest nothing to me that would stop you from getting pregnant. In fact, the fact you've carried a child and conceived naturally suggests you will again. I'll run some tests and we'll set a date to begin."

His words and the certainty behind them that she'd one day become a mother almost dragged the sob from her throat. He couldn't know the scar he was opening with his words or the future he suggested was impossible because the man who held her so tight now hated her. The image they were portraying was a myth, a story.

"Could we take a few minutes, Dr Joseph?"

She heard Noah speak and blinked the sting from her eyes, as she tried to swallow past the glass in her throat. "No, it's fine. I'm okay." She knew her smile didn't fool Noah but he let it go, as did Dr Joseph. "May I use the ladies first, though?" She needed to remember why she was there and not allow the past to ruin her sister's life.

"Yes, it's through that door on the right. I'll meet you both back in my office."

They watched Dr Joseph walk away before Noah pulled her into the disabled toilet and closed the door. "Are you alright?"

Charlie nodded but didn't answer him.

"Damn it, I should never have put you in this position. It's too much."

Her hand reached for his arm, and he paused, his eyes on her, his breath coming fast. "No, it was harder than I thought, but I'm okay."

"How can you say that? I know you, Charlie."

He did know her, and she knew him, which was why she knew this was as hard for him as it was for her. "Do you think about him?"

Her question seemed to catch him off guard, but he dropped his head nodding slowly. "Every single day."

"Me too."

The admission was torn from her throat and his hands came up to cup her shoulders. His eyes closed in pain as she buried her face in his chest. "I'm so damn sorry, Charl."

"It wasn't your fault. It was mine."

"No, baby, it wasn't. I should have been there for you."

"You were, Noah. You would've been the best dad."

"Baby." His voice was laced with anguish.

He held her while she cried, her hand placed over his rapidly beating heart. "Let's get out of here and find a new plan. I can't bear to watch you in pain like this."

"No, let's do what we came to do. Drop the bugs and find the security room."

His hands rubbed her shoulders as they stood in each other's arms. "You sure?"

"Yeah, let's do this."

He studied her for a moment and then nodded. "Okay, baby. Let's go."

The light kiss he dropped on her lips was oh so familiar and so natural that she wasn't even sure Noah was aware he'd done it. Or that he was calling her baby again as he had when they were married. Today had been brutal, so much harder than she'd thought but she'd gotten through it because of Noah. Because he'd been there every step of the way just like he'd always been. She'd just been too broken and guilt-ridden to see it before.

CHAPTER 9

"Was that true in there, what you said about a baby?"

Bishop was sitting outside the Mountain Rescue Centre in a deck chair smoking a cigar. The drive home from Leeds had been quiet for him and Charlie, as they tried to process the feelings the visit brought up. About an hour in, Charlie had fallen asleep, exhaustion forcing her body into slumber.

He cocked his head at Hurricane who blew smoke rings into the cooling night air. It was only the two of them who indulged in this ritual and for him, it traced back to his adoptive father who'd only ever smoked the occasional cigar. The sweet smell was a memory he'd needed tonight after the gut-wrenching day they'd had.

True to her word, Charlie had pulled strength from somewhere and they'd managed to plant the bugs and drop a device in the security room that would help Watchdog access the systems undetected without anyone getting caught.

He looked across the vista, seeing lights in the far distance but not hearing a sound, the peace and tranquillity of these mountains a balm to his bruised soul. "Yes."

"I'm sorry. I had no idea."

"No reason you should. I don't talk about it."

"I get that. Some things are just too hard, right?"

Bishop looked across at his friend who so often hid behind laughter and jokes, the same way he did and recognised a similar pain in him. "You lost someone?"

Hurricane shook his head. "Not someone, something. My career."

He looked at him with sympathy in his eyes and it almost dragged Bishop under. "Want to talk about it?"

"Fuck no."

"Wanna see if Val left any food?"

Hurricane bent forward and rubbed the end of his cigar against the ground to put it out before standing and making sure no embers were left. "Hell, yes."

The two men made their way back inside to the kitchen but were disappointed to see no food was left.

"Guess I'll head to my place and see if I can raid my own fridge."

Bishop wanted to check on Charlie first though, so said good-night to Hurricane and headed toward her apartment door. Stopping, he paused and wondered if he should just leave but as he was about to leave the door swung open behind him.

"Noah."

"I wanted to check on you. See if you were okay."

Charlie pulled the door shut behind her as she stepped out, putting her body closer to his. Her scent tickled his nose, and he fought the urge to inhale like a creeper.

"I was actually coming to find you to thank you for earlier. Today was harder than I expected it to be, and you were great."

Bishop shoved his hands in his pockets. "No problem."

He couldn't help thinking that although it had been hard earlier, it had also felt natural. Supporting her, holding her, kissing her, touching her, as opposed to this awkward peace treaty.

"You want me to rustle up some spag bol?" He didn't know where the invite came from and he knew it was a mistake. But when she flashed him a smile, the dimple in her left cheek showing, he felt a hundred feet tall and knew he couldn't take it back even if he really wanted to. That was what Charlie did for him, she made him feel like someone worth loving until she hadn't.

Walking side by side they headed toward his apartment, and he let them in, throwing his jacket on the couch as he passed.

Taking out the beef mince he began to assemble everything he'd need, laying the vegetables on the counter.

"Need some help?"

"Sure, you chop, I'll wash."

They worked together, him washing the veg as she chopped and added it to the pan as if no time had passed at all. The silence between them wasn't easy like before but it wasn't filled with hatred either. Sometime between the pub and now, his feelings had eased.

"Would you like a drink? I have red or white wine or beer."

"Red would be good, but only a small one."

Bishop poured the wine and got himself a beer as she washed her hands and headed to the other side of the counter to watch him cook like she'd done a hundred times in their marriage.

"So, apart from getting fired, what else have you been up to?"

Charlie looked up from where she'd been rolling her finger around the rim of her glass. "Not a lot. Work, work, and more work. I went to see my dad after Andrea left but he was busy."

"Asshole," Bishop said into the rim of his bottle, his disdain for the man who'd abandoned his child no secret to Charlie.

"Yeah, you never liked him."

"Because he treated you like shit."

"You can't choose your family, Noah."

"Bullshit. You can." Bishop sighed as he dropped the bottle to the counter and turned to stir the pasta.

"At least he was sober."

Bishop spun back around. "Charl, you can't rate people's treatment of you based on the fact your mother was an alcoholic and might have been worse. He left you with her and that's worse. She

63

was ill. He was just a rich asshole who didn't want his life disturbed by a child."

"Wow, don't pull your punches, Noah."

Bishop plated up, angrily slamming the pan down before brandishing a wedge of parmesan like a weapon at her. "Cheese?"

"Yes."

They were back to angry again and he hated it. Eating in silence, he watched her push her food around the plate before taking a few bites, then pushing it away.

"Listen, maybe we should talk about the elephant in the room first."

He hadn't expected her to bring it up, but she was right. If they were going to do this, they needed to get whatever was still smarting like a splinter under a fingernail out in the open.

"Okay." He crossed his arms over his chest. "Why did you shoot me and leave me for dead?"

"I had no choice."

Noah rolled his eyes. "Of course you'd say that. But we both know that's bullshit. I get you wanted to maintain your cover, but we had what we needed to take Armand Vernier down."

"No, we didn't. A few bribes here and there and the evidence would've disappeared, and you know it."

"Then we would've gone back and tried again."

"Noah, if I hadn't shot you he would have. He had a sniper pointed right at you."

"I know and I get that but why leave with him? I was dying and you walked away as if I meant nothing to you."

"Come on, Noah, you know that isn't true."

"Isn't it? You didn't seem to have any trouble doing it. You skipped off happily to handle your case and left me to it. I bet you were gutted when I lived and you had to actually divorce me."

Charlie threw her hands in the air. "You're impossible."

"I'm impossible? You're the definition of impossible. One minute you couldn't get enough of me, the next you were shutting me out. Acting as if I was to blame for everything."

"That's not fair. I never blamed you."

The conversation had de-escalated fast from the shooting to what he knew was the real issue. "You blamed me for not being there when you went into labour."

"No, you blamed yourself for that."

Noah strode toward her, stopping just shy of touching her. "Liar."

Charlie was breathing fast as her hand came up and the slap he'd been expecting stung across his face. "Bastard."

"Shrew."

"I hate you."

"I fucking hate you, too."

Then she was in his arms, and he was kissing her. It was hungry and punishing, the emotions too close to the surface to be anything less than explosive.

He backed her up to the wall, knowing as he did it was a mistake. But try as he might, he couldn't find it in himself to stop.

Her hands tore at his buckle as he stepped back to rip his shirt over his head and toss it to the side. Her eyes were wild with lust and heat as she shrugged out of her shirt and tossed it behind him. Her hands grabbed for him, and he lifted her in his arms, his hands under her ass, as he kissed her with a punishing brutality that was almost healing.

Her hand freed his rock-hard cock and stroked from root to tip, making him growl in response. He was so turned on he could blow his load just from that, but he wanted to be inside her too bad to allow that to happen.

Dropping her legs for a second, he helped her remove her jeans and panties, revealing the smooth pussy he'd lost himself in so many times. He felt consumed with feelings, his body on fire with desire for her. It was madness, and he'd gladly give into it before he'd stop this.

Lifting her once more, he positioned himself at her entrance feeling her desire coat the tip of his cock. "So fucking wet."

"Stop talking and fuck me, Noah."

He pushed in fast, her walls gripping him so hard he closed his eyes and had to recite the periodic table to stop himself from coming.

A moan tore from her throat as he began to fuck her, his body slamming into her hard, over and over until he knew it would leave marks on her skin and he couldn't bring himself to regret marking her as his. Charlie gripped his hair, her nails skimming over his body as he drove them both towards madness.

Dipping his head, he sucked a pert nipple into his mouth through the lace of her pink bra.

"Oh, oh."

"That's it, baby, milk my cock."

Her climax seemed to hit her fast, choking out a series of breathy curse words from her sexy lips.

"So fucking hot. Again."

His mouth on her nipple, his thumb over her swollen clit, he fucked her hard, not letting up after her first climax until she was moaning and thrashing her body as the next took them both down.

His balls tightened, pleasure sizzling up his spine as he came so hard he saw stars. On and on it went as he jerked against her, feeling her pussy walls clench around him. Noah kissed her neck as he caught his breath, trying to summon up the energy to stand without her support or the wall behind her.

After a few minutes of holding them both in the moment, he let her down and realised with horror that they hadn't used protection. He was so used to being together with nothing between them that he hadn't even considered it. "Fuck, we didn't use a condom. I'm so sorry, Charlie."

Charlie stilled as she pulled her jeans up her legs, her skin flushed and red from his beard and touch, making her look sexy as hell.

Riddled with guilt, he hung his head and rubbed the back of his neck. How could he be so irresponsible? He'd let her down once again.

"It should be fine. It's not in the window."

"You're not on contraceptives?"

Charlie shook her head not meeting his eyes. "No reason to be."

Bishop felt like a dick but the knowledge she wasn't sleeping with anyone else made him want to beat his chest and declare himself the winner, which was an incredibly dickish thing to do. "Okay. Well if anything comes from this, we'll deal with it together."

He felt inadequate saying the words but what else was there to say? For him to keep saying he was sorry wouldn't cut it, he'd fucked up again. One more time he should've protected her when he hadn't. "I'm sorry, Charl."

Now dressed, she ran a hand over her hair to try and tame the wildness he loved so much. "It takes two, right? I should have been more careful, but I guess I wasn't expecting that."

Noah laughed without humour. "Me either. It was probably a mistake."

"Agreed, but it's done now. Let's just move on so we get this done and go back to our lives."

The way she said it made his belly clench because she was right. The problem was he'd never wanted her out of his life although it seemed she still did, and that hurt more than any bullet ever would.

CHAPTER 10

A MISTAKE, THAT'S WHAT HE'D CALLED IT. A GOD DAMN MISTAKE. CHARLIE lay in the bed of the apartment Noah had walked her to last night after their disastrous and oh so delicious evening. It had been like a roller coaster she couldn't get off, going from fighting to fucking in seconds.

The sex had been spectacular but then it had always been that way with her and Noah. From the first time to the last, they'd had a connection that was so natural and perfect it was as if they'd been made for each other. The awkwardness and the fighting had been new though and she hated it. She hated even more that it was her own doing.

From day one they'd shared an easy flirtatious banter, but they'd been friends too. He got her, he understood her past, and she'd been the same for him. They'd been each other's person. Yes, they'd fought but it had always been over silly things, and it had been hot and over quickly.

A smile traced her lips as she thought of all the times they'd made up after a silly argument. She sometimes thought the banter was part of the fun, and she wouldn't change that, would never have changed it. Yet she had, she'd taken what they'd had and thrown it away.

Turning to her side, she blinked away the gritty feeling of exhaustion making her eyes sting. Sleep would come eventually, but it wouldn't be restful, it never was these days. It was either filled with images of Noah on the ground dying or...no, she couldn't allow her mind to go to him.

Her body felt numb as she rubbed a hand over her flat tummy, bringing her legs up to ease the pain she felt. The doctor said her pains were psychosomatic, in her head, part of her grief, but they felt real. The only time she didn't feel them was when she was busy working or earlier with Noah.

So she pushed on, working until she dropped, trying to eat what she could when her appetite allowed it. That was something else she'd lost, her love of food. Now it was something she tolerated to keep herself alive.

A memory of her taking a burnt turkey out of the oven the first Christmas she'd shared with Noah made her smile. She'd been so keen to impress him and mortified that she'd managed to ruin their first Christmas together. Noah had simply taken her hand, grabbed crackers, cheeses, and an assortment of cold meat from the fridge and dragged her back into their bedroom.

He'd made love to her all day, and in between, they ate their bed picnic and he told her it was the best Christmas he'd ever had. Those were the tiny things she loved about him, how he could turn any situation from bad to good and show her his love in a million different ways.

Noah was her one and only and he'd made it clear tonight was a mistake. Sure, she'd said it first but that was a protective reaction from the pain. A bigger part of her had wanted him to fight for her and tell her she was wrong, that they could work it out.

How wrong could she be? He was probably cursing himself for touching her. Despair and regret were lonely bed fellows.

Swinging her legs out of the comfy bed, she felt exhaustion pull at her body, making it feel weighed down.

Slipping jeans up her legs, she pulled on a white t-shirt and re-fastened her hair into a ponytail. Maybe a walk around the compound would help get her mind off the nightmare her life had become.

Bás had told her she was free to move around as she saw fit, but not to go into the tech room unless Watchdog was there. Apparently, he was very particular about his things and didn't like anyone touching anything.

Walking past Noah's apartment door, she paused for a second wondering if she should apologise but decided against it. She'd done enough damage already, perhaps some emotional distance would be best.

A grunt coming from the gym made her step falter and a blush creep up her cheeks as she wondered if perhaps she'd caught someone doing something they shouldn't. A thud and another grunt had her blowing out a breath of relief.

Pushing open the door, she saw Duchess bouncing on her feet and jabbing at a punchbag. She wore short gym shorts and a bra top, her body littered with tattoos, and she was stunning. She was one hundred percent heterosexual, but if anyone could make her re-think that it was Duchess.

"You gonna just stare or are you coming inside?"

Charlie liked her despite the cool welcome she'd gotten from her. She liked that Noah had people in his life who'd go to bat for him. He hadn't had enough of that, and the thought released some of the tension inside her. "It's late." Charlie walked around so she wasn't talking to the woman's back and watched her jab again, one, two. Sweat dripped down her face and neck.

Stopping, she caught the swinging bag and faced her. "Thank you for that, Captain Obvious."

Charlie laughed, a natural response to the sarcastic reply. She respected that and it was a nice change from people who knew her

70

treating her with kid gloves. Not that there were many in her life, just Andrea and a few friends from MI5 that she hadn't seen in months. "Yeah, I guess it was kind of obvious."

Duchess eyed her up and down, her expression wary as if she wasn't sure what to make of her.

"You can ask, you know."

Duchess let the bag go and stepped back, her eyes on her gloves as she pulled them off with her teeth and began to unwrap her hands. "So why did you do it?"

"That's a complicated one."

Duchess cocked her head in a challenge. "Try me."

Charlie hauled herself up to sit on the edge of the raised fight ring, looping her body through the rope and leaning forward.

She'd never told a soul why she'd reacted as she had, not even her case worker or Jack, but she found herself wanting Duchess to understand. The words almost bubbled out of her without her conscious thought. "The night I met Noah was like being hit by lightning. I never had a lot growing up. My mum was an alcoholic and I spent much of my time making sure she hadn't choked on her own vomit or got herself into some shit she couldn't handle. The rest of the time I was trying to put food on the table. When she died I joined the army. It seemed like a good idea. I was smart, could look after myself, and it guaranteed I'd never go hungry again."

Charlie watched Duchess take a long pull from a bottle of water and pull herself up to sit next to her. "A few years in I was approached to join MI5 as a case officer. I met Noah and it was like nothing I'd ever known before. It might sound crazy and cliché but he was the missing piece of me. He felt the same and we married and were stupidly happy. He was everything to me. Not just my husband but my best friend. We were a team. It was us against the world."

Sadness swept over her, time seeming to stand still as memories flooded her, both happy and sad. Her fingers closed around the neck-lace she wore with her wedding and engagement rings attached. A piece of her past she just couldn't let go of. "Anyway, after a while we got pregnant and we were both thrilled." Her voice broke off, as she remembered the hope and excitement as they waited for the line on the test. Noah had been as excited as she was and went to every scan and appointment.

"What happened?"

"It was all fine until Noah had to go away for work. I was on office duty by then so couldn't go anywhere. I'd asked him to build the crib, but he'd gotten busy and forgotten. I decided to do it and realised I needed a certain tool. I couldn't find it so went looking in the garage. It was on a top shelf and I climbed on a chair."

Charlie watched Duchess close her eyes, her long lashes black against her creamy skin.

"I fell and the next day went into labour at twenty-seven weeks. Freddie lived for twelve hours and was perfect in every way but he didn't make it. I blamed myself for falling and being so irresponsible, and Noah blamed himself for not protecting us."

"I'm sorry."

Charlie shrugged, swallowing past the angry bees in her throat. "Instead of turning to him, I shut him out. I've never known pain like it. I felt like I was dying each and every day. It made me reckless and paranoid. I knew I couldn't live if something happened to Noah, so when we got that case I threw myself into it. When Armand's men made him and beat him almost to death, I knew they'd shoot him in front of me to try and prove my loyalty. I was undercover as Armand's assistant. I'd worked every day for almost six months trying to take him down. There was a sniper on Noah when they threw him in front of us. I knew if I took the shot he had a chance to make it out somehow."

"Noah didn't want you staying in without him?"

Charlie shook her head. "No, he believes I should've broken cover and called in back-up."

"Why didn't you?"

Charlie swallowed not wanting to reveal too much of Noah's past but knowing she needed to finish this confessional she found herself in. "Armand had an insider at MI5. They'd blown Noah's cover but not mine. I needed to figure out why and who. If I'd called it in, we would never have known, and Noah would never have been safe."

Charlie turned to Duchess. "You have to understand, I couldn't lose anyone else. Noah alive and hating me was better than knowing he no longer breathed the same air as me."

She saw sympathy on the other woman's face. "Does he know?"

"No, I couldn't tell him, or he would've gone scorched earth to protect me. After Freddie, he got so overprotective, and I hated it because it was my fault we lost him."

"So you let him believe you chose the job over him and then divorced him?"

"I guess."

Duchess jumped down and shook her head. "You should tell him. He deserves to know."

Charlie shook her head. "And have him blame himself for that, too? No, I'd rather him hate me than feel guilty."

"Listen, I don't know you but I know Bishop. He still loves you and I think you feel the same."

Charlie reared back in shock. "You're kidding, he hates my guts." She pointed at herself. "She-devil right here, remember?"

"Maybe, but I don't think the kind of love you described to me dies that easy."

"Oh, believe me, it doesn't, but I've hurt him enough. I just want my sister safe so I can let Noah move on."

"Well, that we can help with."

Duchess smiled and it transformed her scary façade into a beauty that was almost blinding.

"What about you? Why are you in here pounding that bag in the middle of the night?"

Duchess waved a hand in the air. "This case I've been working for what seems like forever is driving me crazy and so is the man I have to work it with."

"Oh?" Charlie waggled her eyebrows, feeling more relaxed now that she'd shared her deepest darkest secrets and survived.

"Not like that."

Charlie grinned but she wasn't so sure Duchess was being honest. Perhaps she wasn't the only one with secrets that kept her awake at night.

CHAPTER 11

B<small>ISHOP STEPPED BACK, TURNING AS HIS BACK HIT THE WALL OF THE HALLWAY</small> outside the gym. His legs felt numb as he listened to Charlie spill her guts to Duchess, admitting everything that she couldn't say to him. His thoughts felt scattered as he shamelessly listened to her tell his friend why she'd shot him. A thousand feelings shot through him so fast he couldn't process them.

As he heard movement in the room, he knew he couldn't face Charlie right then, not with this new knowledge and not before he could process some of it at least. Walking quickly back to his apartment, he entered and leaned against the door, needing the support for his weak body. His chest felt tight, and he wondered if he was having a heart attack. Leaning forward with his hands on his knees, he dropped his head and tried to draw in air that felt hot and thick.

Jesus, he was having a damn panic attack. Closing his eyes, he fought to control his breathing. Smell the flowers, blow out the candles. Repeating the mantra his mother had taught him when he was younger and would wake from a nightmare.

He hadn't thought of his adoptive parents in a long time, but now the woman who'd raised him with such love and compassion

75

grounded him and allowed him to battle the blackness that had almost overwhelmed him.

He'd been edgy after he and Charlie had sex, his body craving more of her like a drug addict wanting his next fix. He'd known, or at least he should've known, that having her once would never be enough. She was in his blood, a part of him he couldn't cut out like he did all the other painful things in his life. Her response to minimalize what they had shared cut him off at the knees. When she'd agreed they'd made a mistake, it was like being punched in the gut, rejection like ice water in his veins.

Making it to the couch, Bishop let his muscles give out as he sank down. Exhaustion wrapped around him like a weighted blanket, but he knew he wouldn't sleep. He had so many questions he needed to ask her, and they were playing like a movie in his head, each scenario bringing up a new theory.

Why did she push him away? Did she regret the way they'd ended or that they'd ended at all? It certainly sounded like she'd still loved him if she couldn't bear the thought of him dying. Had they caught the mole inside MI5? Was there any hope they could fix the mess they'd made and find a way back to each other?

The last thought brought him up short. Did he want that? Could he take that risk and open himself up again? He wasn't sure he could and that was why he needed this time to think things through and perhaps see if they even had anything left to salvage. Love wasn't always enough, it sure as hell hadn't saved his son.

Rubbing his hands on his knees, he pushed away those thoughts, not able to think of Freddie for too long or he'd be a mess on the floor.

Instead, he considered everything he'd heard about the reason for the shooting and circled back to the mole at the agency. His fists clenched at the thought someone had lined their own pockets, most likely with blood money, and in the process ruined his life.

As he leaned his head back on the couch, his eyes closed, he couldn't stop his brain from hearing the anguish in Charlie's voice when she'd described losing Freddie. He'd known she blamed herself, but she never should've been in that position to start with.

Sitting forward sharply, he let his elbows rest on his knees as he thought of his son, allowing his mind to remember every single perfect feature for just a moment. A child he'd loved from the minute he'd become a sliver of a possibility. He'd made so many unspoken promises to his son and broken every single one of them and, more, he'd let his wife down.

How had he not seen how much Charlie was suffering and how much pain she was dealing with? He'd seen how reckless and desperate she'd become over her job after the loss but hadn't known how to help her. Instead, he'd let her get it out in what he thought was the best way. Wiping a hand over his face he got up and walked to the cupboard beside the fridge. Grabbing the cheap vodka he kept for such occasions, he poured two fingers, relishing the burn as it went down.

He now recognised the truth. He'd seen it, had felt that creeping fear of losing everything in the pit of his gut and hadn't had a fucking clue how to fix it. Each day had been a round of arguments or snapped words at each other as they'd tried to navigate their grief. Instead of coming together, they'd pushed each other away until, in the end, they didn't know how to be together at all.

In the last few weeks before the shooting, they'd been like strangers passing in the night. Sex was the only thing that had been good between them and even that had a frenzied edge to it. Each clinging to the other in the only way they knew how.

Slamming the glass down on the white quartz counter, he cursed as he thought of how he'd fucked her tonight without protection. Rutted her like she was nobody, not taking the time to worship her like she deserved. His Charlie, the love of his life, and once again he'd put her in a position of vulnerability.

She deserved better than that, better than him, and he'd always known it. Had that self-destructive attitude he'd nurtured grown and poisoned what he'd had?

Sighing, he put the glass in the sink. He couldn't say he had it all worked out. He had no clue how he was going to broach this with her, but there was one thing he needed to do, and that was to get his head out of his ass. He'd reacted after the shooting like a child, seeing the worst in her when he should've stopped and asked himself some difficult questions, like why she'd done it. He hadn't trusted her and that was the crux of the matter. He'd come to expect the worst and closed himself off and reacted when he should've found her and confronted her.

Knowing he wouldn't sleep, he headed toward the tech room to see if anyone was around, his eyes peering into the doors he passed to see if he could see Charlie, but she was nowhere to be found.

Hopefully, after talking to Duchess she'd gone to try and get some sleep. He hadn't heard the entire conversation, too shocked to hear any more for fear of how he might react.

Finding Watchdog at his station, he pulled up a chair next to him and grabbed a handful of the chilli peanuts his friend seemed to live on. "Find anything?"

Watchdog didn't take his eyes off the screen as he shook his head. "Not yet, but I will. I'm close, I can feel it."

Bishop smirked. "Sure that ain't herpes, man?"

"Did you know that as well as the mouth and genitals, you can get herpes infections in the cornea of the eye? If left untreated, it can leave you blind."

Bishop's lips turned down in a grimace. "No, I didn't know that, and I wish I still didn't. Thanks for that visual."

"You started it."

"Yes, I did, and I'm truly sorry for that now."

Watchdog shrugged, but Bishop saw the smirk on his face. The bastard had done it on purpose, his brain full of a million facts from the tomes he read as fast as a mortal read a magazine. Still, he was one of Bishop's favourite people in the world and he'd helped him more than he'd ever know when he first got there. The crazy facts he spouted distracted him from his own troubles. "Anything I can do to help?"

"Fresh coffee would be good."

Bishop saluted as he stood. "Aye, aye, captain."

Watchdog smirked but didn't react other than that. The man was a machine and without a shadow of a doubt, the cleverest person he knew. Social he was not, at least not outside of their group. His story was a mystery and he respected that; God knew they all had one to work here.

Brewing the fresh coffee, he waited for it to percolate as he stuck his head in the fridge.

"Find anything interesting in there?"

Bishop's head shot up and he smacked it on the door as he jumped. Charlie was smiling, her hands in her pockets as he faced her.

"Jesus, you scared the shit out of me."

"I can't believe I got the jump on you."

Bishop rubbed his head where he'd hit it. "Me either, but then you always could." Charlie smiled and it was forced but he could see the effort she was making to call a truce. "It's those tiny, baby feet you have."

Charlie snorted then blushed, showing him a glimpse of the woman he'd first met. "I do *not* have baby feet."

"Darlin', they're tiny."

Charlie waved her hand in the air with nonchalance. "Whatever, better than those clod hoppers you have."

Bishop chuckled, scrubbing a hand down his face to hide his elation that they were back to the friendly banter they'd once had. "I can't apologise for the size of my feet. You know what they say... big feet big...."

"Head?" She crossed her arms pushing her perky breasts closer to the edge of her t-shirt and he glimpsed a chain hanging low.

"Yeah, head," he answered his voice thick with lust again.

Charlie's eyes narrowed, recognising the sound before she spun around. "This place is amazing. The private sector is clearly the way to go."

"It is pretty special here."

"So, what are you doing up still?"

Bishop didn't want to admit that he couldn't sleep because of her, so he shrugged. "I thought I'd help Watchdog."

"Can I help?"

"Sure. Can you grab this while I get the coffee mugs?" He handed her a load of snacks he knew Watchdog would devour throughout the night, protein bars, some nut-ball things that tasted like sawdust, and a pack of chocolate Hobnobs.

"Still a sucker for a Hobnob biscuit?"

They walked side by side down the hall, her shoulder brushing his arm as he opened the door for them to go in with the three large mugs balanced. "The King of biscuits."

"Did you know the name Hobnob comes from the verb 'to hobnob'? Which means to spend time being friendly with someone important or famous."

Charlie blinked and moved closer to Watchdog, a smile teasing her mouth. "Did you know if you laid all the Jaffa Cakes eaten each year in a line, they'd stretch from the UK to Australia and back?"

Watchdog stopped typing and turned to face Charlie with a smile on his face. Bishop stood back and watched, his arms folded after placing the mugs down. He'd forgotten what a trivia geek his wife was.

"Did you know the humble biscuit was the first food to reach the South Pole with the explorer Roald Amundsen in 1911?"

"I actually did know that."

"Bishop, how could you call this woman a she-devil? She's a positive delight."

Bishop facepalmed. "Way to throw me under the bus, asshole." He dared a peek at Charlie but saw her laughing at his embarrassment.

She leaned closer to Watchdog, laying her hand on his shoulder.

"It's fine. It's nothing he hasn't called me to my face and I kind of deserve it. I did shoot him after all."

Bishop clenched his jaw, his back teeth grinding together as he watched her hand on his friend's shoulder. It was an innocent touch, but he couldn't control the growl that slipped past his lips.

"Um, you're gonna need to stop touching me. I might need my balls one day and I think Bish is about two seconds from ripping them off."

Charlie glanced at him in surprise as she dropped her hand, her lips forming a perfect O that made his dick go hard.

"Shall we get to work?"

He turned his back on his wife and friend and pulled up a chair, hoping to calm his nerves before he did something monumentally stupid.

CHAPTER 12

Charlie laid a hand on her stomach, the gap in her waistband already feeling tighter. "Uh, I feel like such a glutton, eating that whole pack of biscuits."

"It's good to treat yourself now and then." Noah leaned back in the chair, the front legs coming off the ground and stretched his arms above his head, allowing the hem of his tee to ride up and give her a glimpse of his muscular abdomen. "Want a picture, Charl?"

A blush stole across her cheeks as her gaze swung to his face to see him smirking at her. God, he was beautiful. "No need. I still have the ones from Spain saved on my phone."

His feet landed with a hard thud as the chair dropped to the floor on all fours. "You do not."

She was crazy admitting this to him but knew she wouldn't lie. Spain had been where Freddie was conceived and a perfect two-week holiday. Sun, sangria, and spectacular sex with the man who owned her heart. "Yep, I do."

"Show me."

Charlie shook her head. "No way, buster." She stood, suddenly having the urge to get some fresh air.

Noah followed and she realised she didn't want to leave his company, the easy truce between them something she didn't want to walk away from.

"Any chance I can get some fresh air? I love this place, but I could do with a walk."

Noah moved closer so he was almost touching her, and she stood her ground, not wanting to back away but wondering if she could resist the urge to throw herself bodily at him. The last few days with the emotion from the clinic and then the wild delicious sex had her craving things she couldn't have.

"Let me just clear it with Bás and I can take you for a walk over the mountains if you like?"

"Oh, I don't want to drag you away from work or anything important."

His hand lifted slowly to cup her chin and force her gaze to his, the amber flecks in his tawny eyes twinkling with an emotion which made her catch her breath.

"You're important, baby."

Tilting her head into his hand she closed her eyes and just let the perfect moment wash over the chaos of her mind. "Noah." She wasn't sure why she said his name, but he was her anchor, he always had been.

"Take a walk with me, baby. Let me show you the mountains."

It felt like he was asking for so much more, but that was just her desperate imagination, so she would take what she could get. "Okay."

A sigh from his lips blew across her face and her eyes opened as he leaned his forehead to hers and kissed her head gently. "Two minutes, Charlie. Give me two minutes to clear it with the boss man."

Her nod had him releasing her and sprinting for the door, a grin so wide on his face it brightened the room.

As she leaned her ass against the console she thought of the last few days and guilt assailed her that she was enjoying this time with

Noah when her sister was possibly in danger, but there was literally nothing more she could do.

The team had cameras at the clinic now, Watchdog was checking into Dr Joseph and trying to figure out who really owned the clinic. Until they got a lead, she had nothing to go on.

"Ready?"

Her head snapped up to see Noah standing in the doorway watching her. He held out his hand to her and she knew there was nothing that would stop her from going to him. "Do I get the bag over the head again?"

"No, Bás cleared you."

Her eyes flashed to his as they entered the elevator that would take them up above ground again. "Really?"

"Sure, you won't rat us out. We trust you."

Three simple words that almost broke her with the impact they had on her heart. "You trust me? After everything I did?"

Noah reached across the space for her hand and terrified of getting burned she hesitated before clasping onto his and allowing the connection to ease the ache in her chest.

"I trust you, Charlie."

Not knowing what to say in response to that, she was relieved to see the doors of the elevator open. Stepping out she saw climbing equipment hung on hooks and realised where she was. "The Mountain Rescue Centre?"

Noah grinned and she realised she was still holding his hand and pulled back before he could. Tucking her hands into the pockets of her hoodie, she clenched her fist as if to hold in the feel of him.

"Yep, we do some rescues now and then too, but it's mainly a front for what we really do."

"And what is that, Noah?"

"Save the world of course."

Shaking her head she followed him out of the building and the early morning sun that warmed the land with its beauty shone on her face. "You always did have a saviour complex, Noah."

"Pot, meet kettle!"

"That was different."

He held out his hand as she moved to step over a small rock and although she'd been walking rougher terrain, she still took the hand he offered.

"Tell me."

Walking silently beside him, Charlie considered whether she could give him this truth at least. "After we, uh... lost him, I felt lost, unhinged, desperate. It was like having an out-of-body experience. I knew I wasn't acting rationally but I couldn't seem to control it. I felt broken, guilt, shame, regret, and grief, so much grief that I wondered if I'd even be able to keep breathing."

"Baby."

"Let me finish, Noah."

He nodded and kept them walking the narrow path, the fresh mountain air and the peace of this place like a balm to her injured soul.

"Some days I'd look at you and imagine you holding him, see the joy I know he would've given you, and knew I'd taken that away. I loved you so much, Noah, I felt like I was losing you too. When we got into fights, I told myself that I was protecting you by pushing you away. I felt too broken to give you what you needed, so I was a bitch."

"You were grieving a loss nobody should ever have to endure. You still are."

"I know that now, but at the time I was a train wreck. So when I heard Armand threatening you, I saw a chance to save you because I knew I wouldn't survive losing you."

"And yet we lost each other."

"Do you think about that time? Of Freddie?" She said his name and the razors in her throat dug painfully as tears sprung to her eyes.

"Every day. I wonder what he'd be doing now. If he'd look like you or me. What his voice would sound like, how beautiful you'd be as a mother. Not a single day goes by when I don't miss that, don't feel it cut deep."

She nodded because she thought it too. "Do you remember when we decided on his name?"

Noah grinned. "Yep, you got it from one of those baby name books and said it meant Peaceful Ruler."

"He would have been a great man. I could feel it." She looked to the wet ground beneath her boots and blushed. "I'm sure that sounds crazy, that every mother feels her son is destined for greatness, but I truly felt it."

Noah stopped and turned her into his body, resting his hands on her hips. "How could he have been anything less with you as his mother?"

A hiccupped sob tore from her throat but the pain she usually felt when thinking of the future her son could have had eased. Noah's hand came around to cup her head and bring her into his chest as he held her.

"I miss him."

"Me too, baby. Every day and I treasure the time we had with him."

Raising her wet eyes to him, she asked the question that had plagued her. "Do you think he was in pain when he died? Did I hurt him when I fell?"

Noah frowned. "No, he wasn't in pain. You asked the nurse that, remember? She said he was perfect except his little lungs were too under-developed."

"I did?"

"Don't you remember?"

Charlie shook her head. "No."

"You'd had a lot of drugs, so that's probably why. You held him for hours and when your body couldn't hold you up any longer, I held you both." Tears formed in Noah's eyes. "We held onto each other when he took his last breath, and I'll never forget the beauty you gave me for those twelve hours or regret him in any way. They were the most precious of my life and if that's all I got to have then he was a blessing. That's the only way I can get up in the morning, by seeing him for the blessing he was, instead of mourning what we lost."

Charlie sniffed and tried to brush her tears away, but instead her fingers landed on Noah's wet cheeks. "I'm so sorry."

"No, you have nothing to be sorry for. It was a tragic accident. There's no saying it wouldn't have happened even if we'd done everything right. I torture myself daily that I let him down, that I let you down, but as I stand here and explain it to you, I can see for the first time it was just how it was meant to be."

"You thought I blamed you."

"Because I blamed myself."

"I'm sorry I pushed you away."

"It's in the past, Charlie. How about we make a pact to move on and see what happens? No promises or expectations."

The hope that spun dizzying circles in her head almost made her trip on an outcropping of stones. Noah caught her with a laugh and held her in his arms and she remembered for the first time since their son died what home felt like. It was a scary thought because losing Noah once had broken her. She didn't know if she'd survive if he decided they couldn't get over the past and have the future she desperately needed.

"How about friends?"

She saw the way he swallowed what he wanted to say before he gave her the sexy smile she loved so much. "With benefits?"

"Ha, cool your jets, buster. Let's see if this outpouring of honesty and self-reflection lasts before we get our kit off again."

"So that's not a no?"

Charlie shook her head and laughed as the sun hit the sky behind her. "You're a menace, Noah Bishop."

"And you love it."

As he turned to walk them back the way they had come he didn't see the hitch in her breathing or the truth in his words, because he was right. She did love him, every single part of him and always would.

CHAPTER 13

"Briefing room, now!" Bás barked as Bishop walked in with Charlie beside him. Her gaze locked on his with questions, but she didn't voice them, her persona changing into operator mode with the flip of a switch. The open honesty they'd shared on the mountain had cleansed a part of his soul he hadn't known needed it, but he felt hope for the first time in a very long time.

Looking around he saw that the entire team was there, Bein and Lotus were back from the Birmingham Clinic where they'd taken a little more time because they had a waitlist to be seen. After a few clicks of the keyboard, Watchdog had fixed that issue and they'd been seen.

"Okay, everyone, listen up. We have an update and I want to hear what everyone found at their relevant clinics."

"Have you found my sister?"

Bishop fought the urge to reach for Charlie as she sat forward, urgency and hope in her voice. He glanced from her to Bás, already knowing that answer.

"No, we haven't had any sightings of Andrea since the CCTV saw her going into the clinic, but we do think we've found the father of her baby. Or at least a possible contender."

Charlie grinned as she looked at him and then back to Bás. "That's great."

"Not exactly. We believe she's been spending time with a man called Carter Cavendish."

The room erupted in chaos as everyone spoke at once, but he was watching Charlie to see if she knew the consequences of Bás' statement. From the way she paled, she clearly did.

Bás held up a hand. "Shut the fuck up a second."

Everyone went silent in an instant as his boss pinched the bridge of his nose. Looking up he pinned Charlie with a look. "Did you know she was dating him?"

"Of course not. We all know the kind of man Carter Cavendish is. I wouldn't have let Andrea within ten miles of him out of choice."

"Well, it seems she ended up on his radar from the club. These images show her leaving with him on multiple different occasions."

The screen behind Bás showed Andrea, looking way more grown up than the last time he'd seen her, beside Carter Cavendish, the man Duchess was investigating and trying to take down with his brothers' help. The man was a piece of work, known for drugs, trafficking of guns, people, extortion, and God knew what else.

The last images of Andrea kissing Carter, as he held the back of her hair in a painful grip, turned his stomach. He saw Charlie swallow and leaned closer to offer his support. Her eyes moved to his and she smiled, a small grateful movement of her lips that didn't reach her eyes.

"I'm gonna kill him," her words were quiet but not a single person in the room could deny the ferocity behind them.

"Well, get in line, because Duchess here has been hunting him for over a year and he's a slippery bastard."

Charlie glared at Bás and then turned her attention to Duchess, some of the fire dimming from the friendship they'd formed over

Charlie's confession that she still didn't know he'd heard. "I want to be there when you take this bastard down."

Duchess nodded once, her enigmatic gaze never leaving Charlie.

"So, we know Charlie and Bishop spoke with Dr Joseph, and his background suggests he's in the clear, but I'd like to get eyes on him for a few days and see for sure. Bein, Lotus, what did you find?"

Lotus rolled her shoulders. "A whole lot of nothing, except for an excessive amount of cameras. We know the clinic runs late, so it might be worth setting round-the-clock surveillance, but my guess is this is a front. They won't keep the girls there if they're doing what you think, and we currently have no evidence of that."

"I agree. I think round the clock on all three would be the best idea." Bishop rolled his finger around the empty space on his ring finger as he spoke, an unknown tell until he saw Charlie watching him. Moving his hands he looked to Bás, not wanting to show his exposed heart in a room full of people, even if they were his friends.

"Agreed. Bein and Lotus, head back to Birmingham. Val and I will head to London and Hurricane and Duchess will go with you two. Duchess, put in a call to your contact and find out everything you can about this club and any gossip around the girl."

She crossed her arms, tilting her head to the side in thought. "I should probably do this in person."

"Fine. You head to London with us then and Titan and Reaper can go with Bishop, and Charlie with Hurricane. I think given the girl—"

"Andrea, her name is Andrea and I get this isn't personal for you, but to me, it's very personal. So please use her name." Bishop wasn't sure where his outburst came from, but it was out there now and all the eyes in the room were on him.

Bás folded his arms over his chest, adjusting his stance as he watched him with a closed expression. "I'm aware just how personal this is, but you know how we operate, so cool the fuck down. Andrea is a priority to us too. Don't go getting your dick in a dangle over the slightest thing or I'll pull you from this case."

Bishop went rigid at the threat. "I'd like to see you try."

A smirk crossed his boss's face and he wasn't sure why he was goading him this way, only that his body felt itchy in his skin.

"Noah, stop it."

Pulling his gaze away from Bás he saw Charlie looking at him like he'd gone mad. Was this how she felt when she was out of her mind with grief? Like she couldn't control her words or actions even though she knew they were destructive.

"What's going on?" Her hand on his arm made him look down at the touch that had always soothed his soul.

"Nothing is the matter. I just don't want them referring to her as 'the girl'."

Her forehead crinkled like she was trying to read him and all he wanted to do was take her in his arms and turn back time.

"Duly noted." Bás' sharp words broke the spell that had clouded around them. "Bishop, I suggest you head to the club where Andrea worked and see if you can find out more about her and Carter."

"Sure, good plan."

Bás nodded but Bishop knew they were going to be having a conversation soon about his attitude. "Reaper and Titan, I want you to sort surveillance on the clinic and Dr Joseph."

"I'll coordinate with Watchdog on that," Reaper offered, shoving his hands in his pockets.

"Let's get to it."

Bishop went to walk away but stopped at Bás' words. "Bishop, a word."

No please or thank you which meant he was pissed.

Charlie hesitated, never one to leave a man behind until she had. Shaking that thought away he gritted his jaw in anger at himself. Charlie had explained why she'd done it and while he didn't fully understand it, he could accept it hadn't been for the reasons he'd thought.

"Go pack and I'll meet you in the kitchen in half an hour."

"You sure?"

Charlie eyed Bás behind him, looking like she was about to go to bat for him and he winked at her. "One hundred percent sure."

He watched her walk away, her hips swinging, her delectable ass in those jeans the stuff dreams were made of, waiting until she was out of earshot before he spun to face Bás.

"You good?"

Bishop hadn't been expecting that question. He went to answer by rote but stopped at the arched eyebrow from his boss and friend. If he lied to Bás, the man wouldn't think twice about grounding him. "I'm processing a few things and dealing with others."

"Anything you need to share?"

"Not right now."

Bás lifted his chin to the door where Charlie had disappeared. "And Charlie?"

"Let's just say not everything is as I assumed it was. She has her own shit to deal with too and I'm at a loss with how to help her." Bishop grasped the back of his neck and turned away. "Truth is, I didn't help her. I fucked up."

"Bishop, I have no idea what it's like to have a child let alone lose one, but I'm telling you right now, that woman loves you and it's clear as day you love her."

"It's not always enough though, is it? You can love someone more than your own life and still not be able to make it work."

"I won't pretend to know about that either. I've never been in love before, but I can tell you communication is the key. Talk to her, tell her how you feel, and really listen when she speaks. Most people won't give up and tell you what they need. Especially a woman like her who's used to looking after others."

Bishop squinted at Bás, jealousy blasting through him at the thought Bás might know her better.

Holding up a hand he moved closer. "Cool down, I read her file. I know about her mother and her useless piece of shit father." Bás' hand landed on his shoulder. "Talk to her. Don't be afraid to be vulnerable if you want her back. You both went through something awful, and everyone processes things differently."

"What if it's not enough?"

"You won't know unless you try."

"Easier said than done, Bás."

"I never said it would be easy."

"Why are you so invested in this?"

Now it was Bás turn to sigh. "I see how you are together, how you look at her. It's how Sebastian looks at Snow, how Bein looks at Aoife. You'd burn the whole world down to see her smile."

Bishop nodded, slowly realising his boss was right. There was nothing he wouldn't do for Charlie.

"Let's start by finding Andrea, though."

"Good plan."

CHAPTER 14

"What the hell are you wearing?"

Charlie turned toward the doorway of the bedroom she was using at the safe house in Leeds and looked at her ex-husband. His eyes travelled over her legs, up her body, pausing on her ass before moving up to stall once more on her breasts before landing on her face. The heat in his stare almost made her combust with desire. Hooded eyes made her cross her leg in front of her to ease the ache between them. "A dress."

Noah stepped into the room, the sleeves of his black shirt rolled up exposing the corded muscle of his forearms and the watch she'd given him as a wedding present. Surprised to see it, she didn't catch his next words until he growled.

"Don't look at me like that while wearing that scrap of fabric or we won't be leaving this room." Stormy eyes drank her in as he traced an invisible line over her body, making goosebumps break out on her skin.

Turning back to the mirror, her hands shook as she tried to hook an earring in her lobe.

"Let me." Noah took the dangly crystal hoop from her hand and swept her hair back from her neck as he gently inserted the earring. His knuckles brushed the curve of her neck and made her nipples bead. "There."

"Thank you."

His hand swept down her shoulder and arm before he tangled his fingers with hers. Looking at the floor, she knew what she'd see if she looked at him and it frightened her how much she wanted him. They still had so much emotional baggage to unpack and if she allowed hope in, she'd be crushed if he decided he didn't want her anymore.

"You know, I'm going to have to murder every man that looks at you tonight."

Her head flew up to meet his eyes and she felt intoxicated by what she saw there. Naked hunger, desire, ownership, and love all mingled into one molten expression. "Why?"

His finger traced the exposed skin of her thigh in the short dress, and she inhaled sharply, her breath sticking in her throat.

"Because every man in there will be picturing this dress on his floor and nobody gets to see that except me."

"We aren't married anymore, Noah. I don't belong to you."

The words sounded confident but the breathy way they escaped her mouth lacked the conviction she was going for.

Bending his head, he brushed his lips against her jaw in a butterfly kiss and the electricity between them almost knocked her off her feet. One simple, almost innocent kiss from this man was everything.

"You'll always belong to me, Charlie. My heart knows it and so does yours. You're mine."

With that, he stepped back and she swayed forward, locked in an exquisite dream before he steadied her. His eyes swept over her again making her breasts feel heavy and her body ache for him.

Turning, he strode to the door, his ass tight and sexy as hell in dark denim. "I'm fucking getting arrested."

Charlie smirked as he jogged down the stairs.

"Ten minutes, Charlie."

"Be down in five."

It was a pattern they'd gotten into when they went anywhere. He'd remind her of the time and she'd rush to beat it.

Stepping back, she surveyed the short navy dress which clung to her body, the neckline was modest with an asymmetric one-shoulder design. The silver sandals were high but heels had never been a problem for her. She could run in them so that was fine. Her blonde hair hung in waves around her shoulders and her make-up was smoky with nude lips. Had she known the effect this outfit would have on Noah? Not consciously but she also knew him better than anyone and he was a leg man.

Grabbing the clutch from the dresser of the two-bedroom safe house they were using in the centre of Leeds, she headed down the stairs with six minutes to spare.

Noah was waiting at the bottom with her coat, shaking his head and muttering to himself as he helped her into it.

"You know talking to yourself is the first sign of madness."

"The only thing driving me crazy is you, Charlotte Anne Bishop."

Charlie rolled her lips as they got into the car being driven by Titan. "Oooh, you full named me."

Noah rolled his eyes. "Give me strength."

The twitch of his lips gave him away though, and she winked at Titan in the rear-view mirror as he smirked.

This was them; banter and sarcasm were a big part of the fire they'd had, and it felt comfortable and new at the same time. The flutters in her tummy that always happened around her ex-husband had never subsided. She'd just shut them out with all the other joy when her son died and she forgot how to live.

The club was packed as she got out of the car and Noah took her hand firmly in his. *The Venue* was the go-to place on a Saturday night and the queue stretched down the street and around the corner.

They walked up to the bouncer, flashed him the passes they had arranged earlier and the barrier was opened. They headed straight in as the bouncer winked at her and Noah growled.

"Cool it, tiger."

"Why do people keep saying that to me?"

"Maybe it's the steam coming from your ears."

"Still annoying."

Charlie grinned at him as they left their jackets with the coat check. Noah took her hand once more and led her into the club where dance music made the floor bounce from the bass.

Dancers in elevated cages and little clothing performed for the patrons above the dance floor. The bar was two deep, and the main dance floor was packed with gyrating bodies having a good time. Looking up past the dancers, she saw a second level where the VIPs would have their own bar and floor. But it was the men looking down on the people below like they were cattle at an auction which made her skin crawl.

"This place is a meat market."

Noah nodded as he steered her toward the bar with his hand on her hip. "Let's get a drink and see if we can get anything from any of the bar staff."

A blond-haired barman, who was rocking a Mohawk with tattoos on his skull, leaned over. "What can I get you?"

"I'll have a gin and tonic with lime." She glanced at Noah to see him glaring at the barman. "Noah!"

"A beer."

His sullen response almost made her laugh but someone jostled her, sending her flying back against Noah.

His hands tightened around her waist, pulling her close, his body protecting her as he put a hand in front of her to push at the pissed-up college student who had knocked into her. "Fucking watch it, asshole."

The kid laughed and turned to his friends.

"He's just a kid."

"Yeah, well, he should know better."

"Yes, Grandad."

Noah handed over a twenty to the barman and as he handed the change back, she stopped him.

"Hey, buddy, you know this girl?"

Charlie flashed her phone at the man whose eyes went wide before he looked away. "Nah, never seen her before."

"Okay, thanks."

Pushing back through the throng of people they found a corner to stand in and watch the room. Anyone seeing them would assume they were just a couple flirting or trying to hook up. Especially as Noah positioned Charlie between his legs, her back to his front, his hands over her belly possessively. Charlie knew she should hate it but she loved how Noah always kept her close and wasn't afraid to show people she was his. His words from earlier came back to her and she wondered if he'd truly meant it or if it was some sexual powerplay at work.

"So, the bartender was lying."

Focusing back on why they were there she nodded as she played with the straw at her lips to make it look like she was drinking. "Yeah, he was. We should probably do a circuit."

"I guess."

Twisting her neck, she looked up at Noah who was the perfect height for kissing in the heels she wore.

"Come on, grumpy."

Noah walked behind her as she made a slow lap of the club, passing the closed-off VIP section where two burly bouncers stood guard. No getting up there without an invite.

As they passed the restrooms her bladder made itself known. "Hey, I need to use the ladies."

"I'll wait here."

Noah positioned himself at the entrance to the narrow corridor and folded his arms. God, he was handsome and every woman in the room knew it. She wasn't blind, she'd seen the looks he was getting, some subtle, others just downright ogling him. She couldn't blame them. He was hot as fuck and had that dangerous bad boy vibe, which when you knew him was laughable. Noah Bishop wasn't a bad boy, not like that. He was dangerous, no doubt, and he led a life which was the same, but he was a teddy bear with those he loved.

Using the restroom, she washed her hands and was touching up her make-up when a woman came in behind her. She looked like one of the dancers from the cage and she knew she couldn't waste the opportunity.

"Hey, you work here?"

The woman was beautiful, in a hard-knocks kind of way. Slim to the point of being malnourished, she had long, red hair with dark extensions and wore a bra top and tiny shorts. But it was the beaten, hard look on her face, and the tell-tale track marks on her arms which broke Charlie's heart.

"What's it to you?"

"My sister worked here, and I wondered if you knew her."

The instant she said the words the other woman shut down. "Don't know nothin'."

Charlie held out her phone. "Please, will you just look?"

"Listen, lady, I don't want any trouble."

"I won't cause you trouble. Can you just let me know if you've seen her recently? Please?"

On a sigh, the woman looked down and paled as if seeing a ghost.

"You know her don't you?"

The woman stepped back, her hand out as if to protect herself. "You need to leave. That's one of Carter's girls."

"Carter Cavendish?"

"Look, lady, you seem alright, but you don't want to get mixed up in this. Carter won't take kindly to questions."

Charlie nodded. "I understand. Thanks for your help."

The woman left and Charlie took a second to compose herself before pulling back the door to the ladies and coming face to face with two huge men.

"Miss, your presence is requested in the VIP lounge."

She looked toward the end of the corridor, but Noah had his back to her fending off women. Taking her by the elbow, the two men didn't give her a chance to turn down their offer before propelling her in the opposite direction toward the back stairs.

With one man in front of her and the other behind, she had no choice but to follow them. She could take them out, that wasn't an issue, but she had a feeling she'd get more answers by following them into the lion's den.

The upper floor was as she'd expected. A glossy black bar with crystal glasses and an array of top-shelf spirits, a smaller dance floor, and black leather couches where men in expensive suits sat around with glamorous, scantily clad women draped off them like accessories. Seeing the edge of the balcony that overlooked the dance floor, she wondered if she could signal Noah from there and let him know she was okay. He'd lose his mind when he found her missing, but it was short-term, or at least she hoped so.

Approaching four men with their backs to her, Charlie made a note of her exit options, either the way she'd come or over the balcony.

"Sir."

One of the goons pushed her forward and stood back as she tried her best not to turn around and rip his throat out for touching her.

A man she instantly recognised as Carter Cavendish turned his head toward her and offered her a cold but charming smile. "Ah, here she is. The woman asking questions about one of my employees."

Charlie gritted her teeth, digging her fingernails in her palm to stop herself from launching an attack on the man she knew in her heart was responsible for her sister's disappearance. She glanced around to see if she recognised any of the three men with Carter but nothing jumped out at her.

His gaze roamed over her body in a suggestive leer which made her skin crawl. "Please sit. Allow me to answer any questions you may have."

"I don't want to bother you."

Carter stood to his full height, which was around six feet, and buttoned the jacket of what was likely a three-thousand-pound suit. "I insist."

Carter led her toward the bar and ordered two cognacs from the pretty bartender. She needed this information even though she knew it would be mostly lies, but it was what he didn't say which would give her the biggest clue.

"I appreciate you taking the time, Mr...?"

Carter threw his head back and laughed loudly as his hand gripped her elbow, pulling her close. "You're a delight. You may call me Carter."

"Well, Carter, I believe my sister worked here and now she's missing."

The fake furrow in his brow made her want to vomit.

"That's terrible news. Do you perhaps have a picture or a name for this girl?"

He handed her the cognac and brushed his finger over her arm as he did, making his intentions very clear as he undressed her with his eyes.

She shoved the picture under his nose, dislodging the wandering fingers she wanted to break in multiple places. "My sister's name is Andrea. Do you know her?"

He looked down and not a shadow crossed his face before he dismissed her sister. "No, I don't recall meeting her."

"Oh, that's a shame." Charlie bit back calling him out on his lies, knowing men like him didn't respond well to being called out, especially in public.

"Perhaps she merely took a vacation."

"Maybe, but that isn't like her at all."

"Well, young women can be irresponsible and get themselves into all sorts of situations that can lead to trouble they can't get out of. But I'm sure that's not the case for this girl."

Charlie worked through an entire fantasy of spitting in his face and then drop kicking this asshole off the balcony as he looked at her with his snake oil charm. He knew exactly where Andrea was and what had happened because he was behind it, and she'd prove it.

"Lucky for her she has a sister who'll stop at nothing to find her then." Challenge thrown down, she levelled a glare on the man responsible and waited for his response.

"Indeed."

Playing with the ring on his pinkie finger, he let his eyes move over her again as if assessing her before lifting a hand to her hair and fingering the end. "I wish you luck, Miss...?"

"You can call me Mrs Bishop."

"Ah, a married woman. No worries. I don't mind sharing."

"Yeah, well, I fucking do. So take your hands off my wife before I break every bone in your body."

CHAPTER 15

BISHOP FELT MURDEROUS AS HE WATCHED CARTER CAVENDISH OGLE CHARLIE like a piece of meat. When she hadn't come back from the toilet, he'd searched every inch of the club before finding the back entrance to the VIP area. Not having back-up had been a tactical decision and he'd been comfortable with it given the times they'd worked together without it in the past. Until he couldn't find her, then he cursed himself for not asking Watchdog to track them.

Carter Cavendish stepped away from Charlie as two men moved in to cover him. He held up a hand to the man who staggered up the stairs looking like he'd gone ten rounds with Mike Tyson and assessed him, seeing the truth in his words.

Noah's chest heaved with breath as he tried to clear the red from his vision and pulled Charlie closer to him. Just that simple touch had his heart rate returning to normal.

"Sweetheart, Carter was just saying that, unfortunately, he's never met my sister."

"That so?"

"It is, Mr Bishop, and I apologise for my forwardness but your wife is an exceptionally beautiful woman and as she was here alone, I assumed you weren't the type to mind."

"She wasn't here alone. She was with me when your goon squad dragged her up here."

"You misunderstand. I merely wanted to help and as it seems I can't help you, I'll have my men escort you out."

"I can find our way out."

Bishop took Charlie's hand and headed toward the stairs. He was getting them both out of there before he followed through on his threat of earlier and killed someone.

"Mr Bishop."

Bishop clenched his jaw and put his body between Charlie and Carter. "What?"

"Perhaps you should take better care of your wife in future. Anything could happen to a lovely treasure such as she."

His body tensed and he was seconds away from going back and rearranging pretty boy's face when he felt Charlie's hand tighten on his arm. "Leave it."

Only the calm demand in her voice relaxed him. "Don't you worry about my wife, Carter. Better yet, never think about her again."

He didn't hear the reply as he swept them through the club, grabbed their coats, and called Titan to bring the car around. He and Reaper had been seconds away from coming in after he'd called about Charlie being missing when he'd seen the stairs to the VIP area and had a hunch she was up there.

Sliding in beside her he closed the door and sighed.

"Everything okay, Bish?"

Looking toward the front he saw Titan watching him in the mirror, his gaze bouncing from him to Charlie. "Yeah, fine but Carter Cavendish is on to us. He cornered Charlie in the VIP section, so he knows we're coming."

Titan whistled between his lips and eyed Charlie. "You wanted to punch the guy, didn't you?"

His words were aimed at Charlie who nodded. "Oh, you have no idea, especially when he denied knowing my sister. That man is as guilty as sin, and I'm going to dance a fucking foxtrot on his grave."

Bishop's fingers flexed on her thigh where his hand had landed after they entered the car and she laid her hand over his.

Titan looked at Charlie in the mirror. "You can dance the foxtrot?"

"Charlie can't dance for shit, but she sure is a trier."

"Hey, I can dance."

Bishop side-eyed her. "Baby, what was the first broken bone I ever had?"

She bit her lip and blushed. "Your toe."

The last of the rage from the evening left him. "And how did I get that broken toe?"

"I stepped on it in my high heels when we were dancing."

Titan laughed out loud, his cheeks wide as Charlie joined in with her own mirth. "Fine, but I have other talents."

Bishop pulled her closer, his arms around her as he kissed the top of her head. "Oh, baby, you have so many talents."

"Get a room you two."

Bishop smirked at Titan as he dropped them off at the safe house. "I'll update Bás in the morning."

"Sure thing. Sleep well. Or not."

His wink had Bishop raising his middle finger but with no real malice.

Following Charlie inside, he saw her kick off her heels and throw her bag on the little entryway table. Her dress rode higher on her gorgeous thighs, and he wanted nothing more than to bury his head between them and hear her scream his name.

"You're staring."

Bishop blinked and shook his head as Charlie moved into the kitchen without even turning toward him. Reaching into the fridge, she took out two sodas and chucked one toward him as she popped open her own. His eyes were glued to her long neck as she drank like she'd just landed at the only oasis in the desert.

"We should let Bás know tonight. He can put Carter under surveillance too."

"He won't want to split Reaper and Titan, but we can tell him and see what he says."

Charlie placed the empty can on the side and let out a tiny burp which made him remember how embarrassed she always got about bodily functions. She was such a contradiction, so open about some things but so closed off about others. "Why are you so embarrassed by burping?"

Charlie blushed as she pushed off the counter and went to walk past him. He caught her wrist and dragged her back so she was in his arms where she belonged. She tensed for just a second before giving him her weight and leaning into his body, her hands on his chest. He wondered if she could feel how his heart rate rose when she touched him.

"Tell me."

His lips grazed her neck and she sighed. "You know my mum was an alcoholic."

"Yes." He hadn't been expecting this diversion.

"Well, let's just say she wasn't exactly prim and proper. She'd often talk and laugh about her bodily functions with the men she let in the house and try and embarrass me with it. She'd take great pride in doing it when she was sober enough to go to a school parent's evening and I guess it made me the other way."

"I'm sorry, Charlie. I hate that you went through what you did as a kid. Nobody should have to be responsible for a parent like you were." Charlie shrugged as he held her, wishing he could erase her past pain. "How come you never told me about that before?"

"You never asked."

You never asked. Such simple words, but they gutted him with their honesty and innocence. He hadn't asked and he wondered how many other things she hadn't told him or that he hadn't bothered to ask about. "I'm sorry, Charlie. I let you down."

She pulled away to look up at him and he wondered how he'd lived the last few years without her. Charlie was his everything. She had been since the day he'd met her and sensed a kindred spirit.

"No, you didn't. You know I hate talking about that time in my life."

"I know, but I can't help thinking we both should have been a bit more forthcoming about things."

"You mean instead of hitting the sheets every chance we got?"

A sexy twinkle in her eye had his lips tipping up as he let his hands rest on the top of her ass. "Oh no, that was imperative."

"Imperative, huh?"

"Absolutely."

Leaning in he kissed her slowly, her mouth opened for him as he swept his tongue in and claimed her. It was slow and relaxed, the heat burning just below the surface as he angled her head controlling the kiss. A whimper escaped her throat and he swallowed down the sound of her pleasure.

"I missed this, Charl."

"I missed you."

Fire danced in her eyes as she traced her hands over his chest making him shiver. His dick, already hard from the kiss, was like steel in his denim jeans. He captured her bottom lip with his teeth and she whimpered, pressing against him, her nipples begging for his touch.

"I want you, Noah."

His growl escaped his throat as he lifted her, wrapping her legs around his hips and walked them towards the stairs. Her fingers in his hair made him shudder as she kissed his neck. His fingers dug into her ass, the globes the perfect size for his grip.

Laying her down on the bed, he took her arms and placed them above her head, watching her eyes go from blue to that hazy green colour he loved so much. Toeing off his boots, he unbuttoned his shirt and shucked it off his shoulders as Charlie shimmied her dress over her head leaving her in nothing but a tiny pink G-string and a lace half-cup bra. Her nipples were poking through the fine lace and begging for his touch.

Releasing the button on his jeans, he let them fall down his legs as he gripped his cock through his boxer briefs to try and stave off the excitement and causing an embarrassing scene.

"Touch yourself, Charlie."

Her eyes on his dick she slid her hand down over her breasts, her fingers pulling and rolling the tight peaks, making his dick weep pre-cum. Losing the boxers he wore, he gripped the base of his cock and stroked slowly as she watched, her lips puffy from his kiss, open now as her chest heaved.

"Show me that sweet pussy, Charlie."

Her hand left her breast and wandered over her flat belly to the edge of lace which hid the last of her from his sight. Her legs hung off the bed as she inched her hand in slowly, teasing him. He loved watching his girl pleasure herself, but he was impatient to taste her again after so long. The last time had been a quick fuck to relieve the tension between them. This would be him showing her with his body what he couldn't say in words.

Her fingers circled the nub of her clit, and she arched her back in pleasure, a moan escaping her sweet mouth.

"Fuck me, that's hot."

A dirty laugh fell from her lips. "I think that's my line, Noah."

A groan forced its way up his throat as he fell to his knees between her lush thighs and inhaled her scent as he ripped her hand away and fell on her like a starving man. Tearing the thong from her body, he planted his face in her pussy and devoured her. The tangy taste on his tongue almost made him come before he could wring one climax from her.

As she writhed against the sheets, one hand in his hair, the other gripping the sheets, he lifted his eyes to see her watching him and what he saw made his heart soar. Open vulnerability and trust were etched on her beautiful face.

His hands gripped her ass as he lifted her hips to get a better angle as he flicked his tongue over her clit until she rolled her head back. Using one hand to keep her where she was, the other travelled over her channel feeling the wet heat of her arousal as he pushed two fingers inside her and stroked over the spot he knew would tip her over the edge.

Her legs shook as she drew in a breath before a keening cry erupted as her thighs squeezed his ears and she came hard. Noah lapped up her juices, loving every last taste as he gentled his movements and gave her a second as he stood and grabbed his wallet.

Rolling a condom down his sensitive length, he squeezed hard to get his errant dick under control. Sinking to the bed he hooked her knee behind his hip as he notched his cock to her entrance.

Holding himself there he looked at her, his lips inches away from hers. "Are you sure?"

"Yes, Noah, I want this. Make love to me."

He sank into her to the hilt, her tight walls almost strangling him and stilled as her nipples brushed the slight covering of hair on his chest through the lace.

"Lose the bra, baby. Let me see you."

Charlie reached back and unhooked the bra, causing the chain around her neck that had fallen into her hair when she lay back to fall forward. Instantly, he recognised the two bands on the chain. Her diamond engagement ring and the wedding band he'd had made to match.

His heart almost stopped before beginning to hammer as he tried to understand the feeling in his chest. Joy. It was joy and hope and all manner of other things that cemented his love for her and his guilt for assuming she'd betrayed him.

"Noah, you need to move."

A smile peppered his lips as he kissed her and then did as she asked, moving his hips as they found a rhythm which drove them both mad. Lifting on both forearms, he rocked into her slow and steady, watching the pleasure on her face build and build before he changed the movement and dragged her back from the edge.

"Noah!"

Her voice held a desperate tone and he smiled. "What, baby?"

"I need to come."

"Who do you belong to?"

Her eyes went wide as she sensed his game, but instead of conceding, she one-upped him as he'd known she would. His Charlie was nobody's fool and she played to her own tune. As she squeezed her inner muscles around his cock, he thought he might black out from pleasure as his spine tingled. Releasing him, she hooked his leg and flipped him to his back so she was astride him, his cock buried deep inside her.

Her grin made him feel alive as she planted her hands on his chest and chased her own orgasm as he watched, enjoying the show.

"That's it, baby. Ride my cock, take what you need."

Her moan ringing in his ears was the only response as her muscles clenched and she came around his cock. She was magnificent, totally unapologetic in her need. It was the most beautiful sight in the world, and he knew he couldn't give this up ever again.

Gripping her hips, he thrust up into her warm, wet heat, her tits bouncing with each movement of his hips. "Touch your tits, baby."

Her hands moved over her lush, full breasts as his thumb circled the nub of nerves at her centre. Every part of his body began to tingle as he chased his orgasm and as she cried out, her body stiffening, he let go and came hard, his seed spilling into her perfect body.

Bishop's heart pounded loud in his ears as Charlie sank against his chest, her energy seeming to leave her like a light being switched off.

Caressing her back with the tips of his fingers he felt her shiver. "You cold?"

"Nah, just ticklish."

Raising up he kissed her head, loving the feel of her relaxed against his body, his still semi-erect cock inside her. "I need to deal with this condom."

"Hmm."

Bishop chuckled low and untangled himself from the woman who held his world in her hand. "Be back."

Dealing with the condom was something he hated but if it kept her safe he'd do what he had to do. His mind went to a few days ago and the unprotected fuck against the wall. He couldn't regret it. He could never regret being with Charlie in any way, but he was ashamed for not thinking it through and asking the question. The truth was, he hadn't been thinking at all. He'd been driven purely by emotion and instinct.

Finishing up, he walked back into the bedroom to find Charlie sprawled across the bed on her belly, snoring softly. He felt a smile on his cheeks at the sight so familiar and beloved. She'd always crashed after sex, but this time he recognised it wasn't just the sex that had worn his girl out, it was lack of sleep too.

She was too thin, her ribs visible on her slim frame and he knew he had to help her heal and maybe in the process fix things between them. Crawling back into bed, he pulled her across his chest and covered them both before letting sleep take him.

CHAPTER 16

"THERE YOU ARE."

Charlie looked up to see Noah walking through the back door of the safe house. Automatically, she tipped her head up from her seated position at the garden table for his kiss. Firm lips captured her mouth in a kiss that was borderline indecent before he pulled away and looked down at the table. "What are you working on?"

In the past seven days since the altercation at the club with Cavendish, things between her and Noah had changed. They hadn't gone back to how they were before, but they were spending every night together. The sex was off-the-charts amazing but it was the open honesty between them that had changed.

In between searching for her sister, they spent every second together talking about the past, about their childhoods, but never about the future and she knew that was her fault.

Every time Noah tried she shut it down, too terrified he might decide he couldn't take a risk on her again. He'd been wonderful in not pushing her and she loved him for it. She'd always love him.

"Charl?"

"Oh, sorry. Yeah. I was going through my sister's social media again to see if I could find anything."

"And?"

"Nothing."

"Well, I do have some news, nothing big, but Watchdog found the parent company of the clinic and it does tie back to Project Cradle."

"Wow, so this is huge."

"It looks like it's a bigger operation than we thought. There are CIA officers involved, high-level criminals, government officials, and the fact it spans the globe is a worry too. Bás and Valentina are headed to the USA to meet with some of our contacts there and find out what they know. Duchess will take over as lead for now."

"Isn't she undercover with the Elysian Casino group?"

"She is, so she has to be careful."

Charlie sighed and let her hands fall to her lap. "God, what a mess."

Warm fingers brushed her neck as Noah sat beside her. "I know, but we'll figure it out together."

Looking up she saw his blue eyes on her and her throat clogged. "Why are you so good to me?"

"You know why."

"But I shot you."

His lips twitched and he nodded. "That you did, and I only forgot to put the bin out one time."

A laugh burst from her, but it was half-hearted at best. "Be serious, Noah."

"I know you only did it to protect me. I heard you talking to Duchess in the gym."

Charlie stilled, bile racing up her throat and she shot to her feet, her hand over her mouth as she ran to the edge of the garden and lost the contents of her stomach.

Retching until her throat hurt, she felt soft hands scoop her hair away from her face and felt a gentle hand on her back.

"You okay, Charl?"

Nodding, she wiped her mouth on her sleeve and straightened, her heart racing from being sick and the news he knew. "Why didn't you tell me?"

Noah raised a brow. "That I knew?"

"Yes."

"Initially, I was trying to process it."

"And after?"

Charlie crossed her arms over her middle as if she could protect herself from more pain.

Noah shoved a hand through his hair and turned away from her. "I'm not sure I'm at the after stage yet. There was a lot. Losing Freddie, your misplaced guilt, your fear for me, the mole inside the agency, the secrets, Charlie. So many secrets."

"I know, I'm sorry."

He strode toward her, and she waited for the moment when he said he couldn't do this anymore. Taking her hands, he held them to his chest, trapping them against his heart. "I know you are, and you don't have to keep saying it. As perverse as it is, I understand why you did it. We'd lost enough and you were terrified of losing me, so you pushed me away first."

A sob broke free and her eyes stung with tears. Noah wrapped his arms around her and held her to his chest. Keeping her together when all she wanted to do was fly into a million pieces.

"I was so scared, and I shot you."

"I know, baby. It's okay."

"No, I shot you."

"Is that why you won't touch my scar?"

"Every time I see it it's a reminder of the worst thing I've ever done, after climbing on that damn chair. If I had missed, or Jack had been a minute late, you'd be dead."

"Charlie, you never miss and if I'd died it wouldn't have been from getting shot."

That only made her sob harder.

"Did you find the mole inside the agency?"

Charlie lifted her head and looked into his eyes. "It was Carson."

"That bastard."

"Yeah, seems he got into debt, and they extorted him. He was killed before we could arrest him."

"I can't believe we worked side by side with that asshole."

"Yeah, me either. He even came to our wedding."

"Well, at least he can't do any more harm."

Charlie went to move away but he held on tighter, his gaze roaming her face before coming back to her eyes.

"Listen, Charlie, I know you don't want to talk about the future, but I need you to know that I want us back. You drive me fucking crazy sometimes, but I love you. I've always loved you and always will until they put me in the ground." He must have felt her stiffen because he rushed on before she could respond. "I'm not saying we go back to how we were, but I'd love it if we worked on us and see if it's possible."

She was about to respond to tell him that she wanted that too when the sound of breaking glass had them both looking toward the house and reaching for their weapons. The first pop of gunfire had Noah grabbing her arm and rushing to the tree line for cover. Hitting a button on his smartwatch, he shouted an alert to Watchdog that they were under attack.

"We need to get inside and find out who sent them."

Fear pricked at her skin at the thought of Noah going into that fight. "No, it's too dangerous."

"We don't have a choice if you want to find your sister, Charlie."

"Fine, but don't die."

With that, she rushed ahead of him, firing the first shot as a man in black fatigues and a ski mask rounded the back hallway of the small, two-bedroom semi-detached property. He dropped before he could raise his firearm. Jumping over him, she motioned to the front of the property as Noah headed upstairs.

With her back to the wall, she could hear the sound of someone in the kitchen as she moved forward. A bullet flew past as she poked her head around.

"Drop your weapon."

The man on the other side fired again as she ran to the other side of the door to try and get a better angle. Pops from upstairs filtered through her brain with shouts and thumps of people fighting but she couldn't let the fear win and distract her. Noah was more than capable of dealing with whoever was up there. She had to believe that, or she'd be history.

Spotting the man who'd shot at her in the reflection of the stainless-steel toaster, she made her move and took the shot, hitting him in the thigh. As he cried out, she slid across the counter and came to stop above him. "Don't move."

She could see the indecision on his face, sensed the moment he decided to go for the weapon which was just feet from him and fired. The sound of someone behind her had her spinning to find Reaper standing there.

Lowering her weapon, she glanced at Noah who rushed into the room and straight for her. She sagged into his arms when he reached her, her hands moving over him looking for an injury.

"I'm okay. I'm okay." Pulling back she saw a look pass between Reaper and Hurricane as Titan joined them.

"Well, I guess the safe house wasn't so safe."

Reaper frowned at Titan's words, but his jaw tensed as he glanced back at her. "We need to leave."

"Are any of them still alive?"

Noah shook his head. "No, they were all going for kill shots, so I had to act first."

A phone rang and Hurricane answered it. "Yeah. ... Yeah. ... Thanks, man."

He hung up and looked at the group. "That was Watchdog. He called the police off, but we still need to get gone before other goons show up."

"Yeah, let's move to the second location. We can call Duchess on our way."

"No need. She's already blowing up my phone. Says she's on her way and will be here in an hour so she must be taking the chopper."

She saw a look of sadness cross Hurricane's face at the words and wondered what could have prompted it.

Glancing back to Noah, she saw Reaper watching her and the skin on her neck prickled in warning. "What?"

He shrugged his shoulders. "Nothing."

Noah sensed the sudden animosity and stepped closer to her. "What the hell is going on?"

"Nothing, let's go."

Reaper turned but Noah grabbed his arm and spun him back as Reaper shook his hand off. "What the fuck, Reaper?"

"Don't you think it's funny that in the entire time we've been doing this not once have we had a safe house compromised, and now all of a sudden we do?"

Reaper glanced at her and the accusation was clear in his blue eyes.

Noah straightened to his full height and went nose to nose with his friend, his tone was pure grit and ice. "What the fuck are you saying?"

"You can't be that naïve. She fucking shot you, man."

Noah looked wounded as he took a step back as if his friend had punched him in the gut. "You think Charlie leaked our location?"

"I'm just saying it's odd."

Hurricane stepped between them and held up his hands. "Everyone, just calm down. We need to go. This can wait until we're clear."

"The fuck it can. I'm not going anywhere with him."

Charlie stepped toward Noah and laid a hand on his arm, his eyes instantly moving toward her with an apology she didn't need. Reaper, however misguided, was looking out for him and she'd always be grateful he had that. "He's just looking out for you."

"How can you say that? He's accusing you of causing this."

Charlie moved between Noah and Reaper and laid her hands on his chest. "He has his reasons, and I did shoot you."

"Oh, for fuck's sake. Yes, you did but we'd just buried our son. You were so lost, baby. You weren't thinking straight."

Charlie heard the sharp intake of breath behind her and knew the others were hearing about Freddie for the first time. She didn't have the energy to deal with that though, she needed to fix this division before it became a permanent rift. "No I wasn't, but you must see he's trying to protect you."

"I don't need his fucking protection."

She shook her head. "You're wrong. We all need it sometimes, Noah."

Turning to Reaper she saw the shadow of remorse on his handsome face. "I get why you feel the way you do. You just saw me shoot an unarmed man, but I can assure you it wasn't to stop him talking. It was because his gun was a few feet away and I saw the second he made the choice to go for it and handled it. I did shoot Noah and you'll never know how sorry I am for that, but that's between us. I'm not asking you to trust me. I understand that's an ask too far. Just give me enough time to pack my shit and I'll get out of your hair."

Noah spun her to face him. "No, you don't have to do that."

"I do. I won't come between you and your friends."

With that, she ran from the room to stop him from seeing the desolation on her face. She needed to get the laptop she'd been using and her spare gun and then she'd leave. Sagging onto the bed, the reality of the situation hit her. She'd never be able to get past what she'd done. Some things were just unforgivable and at this point, she didn't even know if she meant harming their son or shooting her husband. She was a bad joke and had nobody to blame but herself.

CHAPTER 17

Bishop paced the living room of the old rectory where they'd moved their base after the attack on the safe house. He was livid, his blood almost boiling with fury at Reaper's accusations against Charlie. Luckily he'd managed to convince her to come with them and she was currently in the shower. But he knew the first chance she got she was running.

He'd set up guard duty outside her room in the hopes of stopping her, but also so he didn't have to face his friend. Right now he wasn't sure he'd be able to keep it together.

"Hey."

"Duchess."

She was leaning on the second step of the stairs, arms crossed as she watched him. "I heard what happened."

His spine stiffened, and his body went on alert, every muscle looking for a fight. "She didn't do it."

Duchess began her ascent up the stairs, arms still crossed until she reached the landing where he was patrolling. "I know."

"You do?"

"You heard us talking. You know why she did what she did."

"You knew I was there?"

Duchess cocked her head and he wondered what else she knew. "Come on, Bishop, you know me. I didn't hear you, but I sensed movement in the hallway so checked the cameras. You looked devastated."

"I was. I had no idea she felt that way, or that Charlie still loved me. Losing Freddie just imploded our marriage. I thought she hated me. I let myself believe that she'd betrayed me because it was easier than facing the fact that I hadn't helped her when she was so lost."

"You were lost too, Bish."

"I should have protected her. That was my job. Instead, I let her down."

"You didn't let me down, Noah."

His breath left his lungs as he spun to find Charlie leaning in the doorway.

"I'll see you downstairs in a few. We need a meeting."

Duchess smiled at Charlie and he saw the mutual respect pass between the two women in an unspoken connection of female understanding.

"Don't leave me." The words were out before he could even make sense of them.

"Noah, I never wanted to leave you. You were right. I was lost, and so damn broken. Not just from losing Freddie but from my parents, everything my mother put me through with her alcohol addiction, and the rejection from my father. All of it amassed into a giant meltdown which saw me doing things and being someone I wasn't."

"And now?"

"Now I need to find my sister and put myself back together."

"Where does that leave us?"

She moved forward and her expression held hope and fear and regret, and he just wanted to promise her he'd fix it.

"I want the same as you, but we can't fix each other. We have to fix ourselves first and I have to make amends for what I did to you, and that starts with your friends."

"Fuck my friends."

"Uh, no. Not into group sex, Noah."

His lips twitched as he hauled her against his chest. "Smart ass."

"I think you mean sexy ass."

He gave her ass a squeeze and felt his dick harden between their bodies. "Well yeah, but you can't be all sassy and clever. You know it turns me on and I'm fighting for my life here."

"We, Noah. We're fighting because I've come to see that if we want this to work we need to be a team. Not just at work or in bed but be honest about everything we're feeling."

"How are you feeling?"

"Terrified of losing you, of you coming to the realisation that I'm not worth it."

His lips grazed her cheek. "You're worth it, Charlie."

"Now you?"

"Now me what?"

"Tell me how you feel."

Her head was cocked to the side, and he couldn't think of a single thing to say. "Uh."

"Come on, Noah, you can do better than 'uh'."

He slapped her ass. "Don't be sassy."

"Then tell me."

"I'm wondering what changed your mind about running and if this is a ruse for me to lower my guard so you *can* run."

Charlie rubbed her hand up and down his spine. "I guess I had something of an epiphany in the shower. I ran from my feelings before, and it got me nowhere. So this time, as scary as it is, I want to stay and face things. Even if that involves facing Reaper and his scary, overprotective streak."

"Thank you for not running and for being honest."

Charlie smiled and tugged him toward the stairs by his hand. "Let's go face the music."

He let her tow him along into the room that was now full of Titan, Duchess, Hurricane, and lastly Reaper.

His friend locked eyes with him and he didn't know whether to knock his teeth down his throat for being a dick to Charlie or thank him for having his back.

Bishop locked his knees when Reaper stepped forward and offered his hand. "I'm sorry. I was out of line."

Bishop hesitated a second until Charlie nudged him with her shoulder, then he took the hand and shook. "I know you were looking out for me."

"Yeah, well, I was still a dick about it."

"We can agree on that."

He stepped to the side as Reaper angled toward Charlie, his guard still up despite the apology. "I'm sorry, Charlie. I should never have gone off at you like that. I guess I just over-reacted."

"It's fine, and honestly, I don't blame you. I might have done the same if the situation had been reversed. But for the record, I'd never betray Noah again. I know I have a lot of making up to do, but I'll prove I'm worth it."

"Good, now that's cleared up, let's have a pow-wow and fix this shit. Because if I have to spend another day with Mr Grumpy Knob-head Cavendish, I'll be the one doing the shooting."

Bishop raised his eyebrows at Charlie and grinned as Duchess motioned toward the old wooden table in the rectory kitchen.

"I like her," Charlie stage whispered to him making Reaper cough to hide the chuckle.

"As Bás has left me in charge of you children, let's get a few things straight. Charlie is in the clear. She's not involved in this shit storm in any way apart from being a target. Now we have news, so let me just get Watchdog's ugly mug up on the screen and he can fill us in on everything."

Bishop watched Duchess press a few keys, appreciating her no-nonsense attitude.

"Ah, there he is. Wonderboy, what can you tell us?"

Crowded around the table he saw Watchdog look off to the side of the screen before focusing back on them, his mind always working at light speed. "Well, Carter Cavendish has a serious hard-on for Charlie. He wants her found and dealt with, and from what I hear he's raising hell because he hasn't found her or Bishop."

Duchess nodded. "I heard the same thing."

"Do we have anything tangible on him yet?"

Watchdog was leaning back in his seat but sat forward with a shake of his head. "No, motherfucker is as slippery as an eel in a bucketful of baby oil."

"So what do we have?"

"I'm working on a list of properties. Once I send them through, it would be a good idea to get some surveillance set up on them and see what we have, but I've narrowed it down to four. I've been using drones, but I need actual eyes on some of them as trees are making it difficult with the signal."

"Send it through," Duchess instructed.

"Yeah, will do. Also, I found out Dr Joseph isn't Dr Joseph. He's Dr Junior Nkosi and is a South African national. He was struck off for performing terminations on young girls without parental consent."

"He did have pretty strong opinions about girls having babies they didn't want but I didn't peg him for a bad guy."

Bishop squeezed Charlie's leg in support. He hadn't thought so either.

Charlie looked to Duchess who was biting her fingernail. "Do you want us to go back and see him?"

"No, your cover is blown and we can't risk Carter finding you there. Reaper, you and Lotus go and pick him up after he leaves for the day and question him. Find out what he knows, and feel free to be creative. I'm sick of these fuckers being ten steps ahead of us."

"I want to talk to him."

"Me too."

Duchess cast her glance at him and then at Charlie, her expression a controlled mask. "Fine. Reaper, pick him up and bring him here. We can use the storage shed at the bottom of the pasture."

"Will do."

"Watchdog, anything else we should know?"

"Yes, but I'm not sure how to say this."

"Spit it out."

"The men from the safe house were all known associates of Gideon Cavendish. Seems they work security at one of the underground casinos."

Bishop watched Duchess swallow, her entire body going still at the words. "Understood. Do we know how they found us?"

Watchdog's pause was only a split second, but it was enough to tell him that he wasn't being honest. "No."

"Okay, send those details through and we'll get on it today."

"Sure."

"Oh, Watchdog, have we heard back from Bein or Snow about the other sites?"

"Nothing of note which is what we're seeing here. My guess is they keep anything illegal far away from the clinics so nobody gets suspicious."

"Okay." Duchess hit end on the call to disconnect it, her leg bouncing with energy. "Reaper, Titan, go get the good doctor. Hurricane and I will take the first building and Bish and Charlie can wait for you here."

Reaper was out the door with a final look toward him, which still held guilt and regret. Bishop was happy to let him stew on that a little longer. He may have forgiven him, but he'd remember.

Two hours later, he was walking into the storage shed at the back of the old rectory with Charlie beside him. Dr Nkosi or Dr Joseph as they knew him, was zip tied to the chair, a black cloth bag over his head. His head turned toward the sound of the door opening and he flanked the left side as Reaper took the right. Now that they had his prints, Lotus was running them through a database they had access to, to see if anything else came up linked to him.

He nodded for Charlie to get started. She'd earned the right to lead this as far as he was concerned. Her voice lower, a slight European accent to hide her identity, she began the interrogation.

"Dr Nkosi, we have some questions for you."

The man's head cocked like a weird, nervous sparrow waiting for the cat to come out and play. "I... I don't know who that is."

"Stop the bullshit. We know who you are and what kind of people you work for. Now tell us about the missing girls."

Charlie slid the clip into her firearm and Dr Nkosi flinched, the sound one he clearly recognised.

"I don't know about any missing girls. I'm a fertility doctor. Please don't hurt me."

"Wrong answer."

"I'm a good man."

"A good man who gives terminations to young girls without their parents' consent?"

"No, you don't understand. They begged me. The soldiers. They'd do horrific things to them, and a lot of the girls were barely in their teens. They didn't want to carry babies for these monsters to continue their abuse."

Charlie glanced at him and then at Reaper who shrugged, but his jaw had gone hard. Bishop knew the memories of what his so-called friends had done in the Hindu Kush was still raw.

"How did you get into the country?"

"A man. He paid me to come here. Offered me a second chance to do good."

"What man?"

"I don't know. I've never met him. He said I could have a fresh start here and help lots of people."

"You expect us to believe that?"

The man's head sagged low, and his shoulders slumped. "It's the truth."

"Then what happened?" Charlie stepped closer raising his chin with the tip of the gun. He jumped, almost knocking the chair over, but he and Reaper caught him in time, righting the cheap, wooden chair.

"I was asked to start informing him about certain clients."

"What kind of clients?"

"Young women who were alone and seeking a termination. I was told they'd be given extra help to get back on their feet."

"Did you believe him?"

"At first I did, but then I became suspicious that records were never found for those women. I checked and found several had been recorded as missing."

"Then what did you do?"

"I said I was unhappy about the setup and they said they'd kill me if I stopped. That all the women I was helping would be left with no hope."

"So you carried on."

Sniffles sounded throughout the room, as sweat dripped down the man's throat before disappearing into his shirt. "I had no choice."

"There is always a choice, Dr Nkosi. We sometimes make the wrong one, but you've been given a chance to put some of those wrongs right. Tell us where they take the women."

"I don't know, just that they collect them from the clinic after I put in the call."

"And the girls, do they know they're being moved?"

"Yes, I tell them there's a special clinic funded by the government that can help them with a few days of respite and counselling after the procedure. They're collected after hours but I never see them leave or do the handover."

"How righteous of you."

"I'm not a bad man."

"You are the worst kind, Dr Nkosi, because you don't see yourself for what you are."

"I'm gonna need that number you call."

"They'll kill me."

Charlie gave a short humourless laugh and Bishop crossed his arms to stop himself from reaching out and throttling the man. He'd had a gift and he'd thrown it away.

"What makes you think I won't kill you, Dr Nkosi."

The man whimpered and shifted in his seat. "Please."

Charlie leaned forward. "The number. Now!"

"It's in my phone under monopoly."

"Why that name?"

"Because that was what he said to call him."

Reaper went through the man's pockets and found the phone before grabbing the doctor's hand so he could get his fingerprint to unlock the phone. He nodded when he found the contact and tipped his head to the door. He'd get the information to Watchdog while they finished up.

"Did you ever see a girl called Andrea, Dr Nkosi?"

"Why, yes. I did recently. She was a sweet girl."

Noah moved closer to Charlie as he saw the pain flash across her face. The urge to pummel this fake do-gooder had him clenching his fists. "Did you send her to those people too?"

"She said the father was dangerous and she was scared. I just wanted to help."

"That girl was my sister, and you sent her to the very man she was running from."

"I was trying to help her."

"The world doesn't need your kind of help, Mr Nkosi."

"Doctor."

"No, you lost the right to call yourself a doctor when you sent young women to have their babies stolen from them."

"No!"

"Yes. Those girls never had terminations. They were forced to be human incubators, and when they were done their babies were taken from them and they disappeared. Does that sound like something a man sworn to do no harm should be involved with?"

Her only answer was his sobs as he realised it was over, the dream, the myth. Charlie had pulled the blinkers from his eyes in spectacular fashion.

Guiding Charlie out of the shed, he pulled her to his chest, cupping her head with his palm. "I'll call Watchdog and have someone come and deal with Nkosi."

"How could he do that and think he was helping?"

Bishop shook his head. "I don't know. People are messed up."

Looking up at him from under her long lashes she sighed and then reached up to kiss him. "Thank you."

"For what?"

"Not giving up on me."

"Never, Charlie. I'll never give up on you, ever."

CHAPTER 18

THE LAST FIVE DAYS HAD BEEN A MIXED BAG OF CHALLENGES. REAPER WAS tiptoeing around her, and Noah was like a growly mama bear, protective and hovering. She kind of loved that second part, but she didn't want Reaper thinking she held a grudge. Right now though, she had a bigger problem and no idea who to turn to about it.

"Hey, you okay?"

Charlie blinked an automatic smile tipping her lips as Snow walked into the room. She adored this woman who was part Disney Princess and all the cool parts of the villain.

"Yeah, fine. Just thinking."

Rubbing her hands on her knees she stood and went to get more coffee from the pot on the island, but the smell caused a wave of nausea to sweep over her, further confirming her fears.

"You sure? You've gone an ugly shade of green."

Lotus bounded into the room full of her usual energy and bluster. "Hey, what's the shizz?"

"Charlie doesn't feel well."

Placing a hand over her tummy, she tried to argue that she was fine but every breath she took was to keep from hurling all over the floor.

"Oh no, what's up? Is it catching?"

Duchess walked into the room and took an assessment of the situation before she pierced Charlie with a stare. The battle was lost as Lotus poured herself a coffee and Charlie ran for the nearest bathroom, barely making it through the door before she vomited everywhere.

On her knees, she finally sat back and took the cold washcloth Duchess handed her.

"Does he know?"

Charlie shook her head, not having the energy to speak for a second. Wiping her face she accepted the hand Duchess offered her and stood to splash her face again and rinse her mouth. "I'm not even sure myself, yet."

Duchess crossed her arms and looked at her with a raised brow. Although they were the same age, she felt like Duchess definitely took the protective, motherly role inside the group, as did Valentina.

"Well, let's fix that first."

Duchess went to walk away but Charlie grabbed her arm, fear bitter in her mouth. Duchess stilled, her eyes moving over Charlie as her eyes stung with tears.

"I'm scared."

Duchess' features softened as she wrapped an arm around Charlie's shoulders and guided her out of the small toilet and back toward the kitchen. Lotus and Snow both looked at her, Lotus with a buttered crumpet hanging out of her mouth. Funnily enough, that didn't make the nausea any worse and had her tummy grumbling.

She placed a hand over her tummy at the noise and laughed as everyone focused on her.

"You want me to make you a crumpet?" Lotus offered and Charlie knew behind the bolshy attitude was a kind person who'd taken some wrong paths and didn't know how to right those wrongs or deal with her own guilt. Like always recognised like.

"Thank you, that would be nice."

"So, um, what's wrong with you?" Snow asked from her seat at the table where she was munching on a bag of cheese and onion crisps.

Charlie had wished for someone to talk to and now she had three women, but could she open up and take that chance on these women when she hardly knew them?

"You don't have to say, I'm just being nosey."

Charlie waved her hand at Snow and smiled to reassure the woman. "It's fine, but I'd prefer anything shared in here to be kept between us if you don't mind?"

"Of course. We're here for you. We love Bishop like a brother, but us girls have to stick together and you're one of us now."

Her throat closed at Snow's words, and she tried to fight back tears to respond. "So Noah and I had, um, relations."

Lotus placed the buttered crumpet in front of her. "Sex. You had wild monkey sex."

Charlie glanced up to see the grin on the woman's face. "Uh, yeah, we did that, and the first time was kind of a hate fuck situation and it got out of control and we didn't use protection."

"Oh, I love hate sex. It's the best."

"Oh, yeah. I pick arguments with Seb just to rattle him up so we can have hate sex."

"Don't you get bored of that, though?"

Snow and Lotus both looked at Duchess, who looked like she wanted to snatch the words back.

Lotus pointed at her. "We're going to circle back to that." Zeroing in on Charlie again, Lotus continued. "So this little tummy bug is actually going to grow into a big tummy bug with arms and legs and cute little fingers and toes?"

Charlie bit into the crumpet and sighed as the buttery taste filled her mouth. She chewed and swallowed then nodded. "Possibly. I haven't taken a test and Noah has no idea."

"You're worried how he'll react? 'Cos let me tell you, that man will make a fine father."

Snow's confidence in Noah touched Charlie. "He was. For twelve hours he was the best daddy any child could ask for."

"What?" Lotus shrieked.

Duchess shushed her. "Keep it down."

"What? The guys aren't here. They won't be back for hours yet."

They'd split the jobs up and this turn around the girls had all ended up at home together.

"I know but not everyone is used to your over-exuberance."

Lotus waved it off and focused on Charlie. "Bishop is a dad?"

"We had a son. He only lived for twelve hours but Noah was the best. He held him in his arms and protected him as best he could, talking to him, telling him how much he loved him and then he held us both as Freddie slipped away."

She was so lost in her memories it took a second for her to realise both Lotus and Snow were sniffing as tears ran down their cheeks. "Oh gosh. I didn't mean to make you cry."

Charlie reached for Lotus and Snow and they both descended on her and held her tight as Duchess smiled like a loving parent.

"We're so sorry, Charlie."

"It's okay. It wasn't anyone's fault. I went into labour at twenty-seven weeks and he didn't survive."

Saying it she realised it was the first time she'd talked about this with anyone other than Noah, and the first time she believed nobody was to blame either.

"So now you're terrified to find out. Because that must be a scary prospect, even if it was planned which I'm guessing this wasn't?"

Snow held her hand and Charlie squeezed back to let her know how much she appreciated it. "No, not planned."

"Well, let's find out what we're dealing with first before we panic." Duchess looked at Lotus. "You go to the pharmacy and grab a test before the boys get back."

Snow raised her hand. "I actually have a spare in my kit."

Lotus' mouth fell open. "You too?"

Snow shook her head. "No, but we're trying, and I've become something of a pee on a stick addict."

Lotus grimaced. "Is that a thing?"

Charlie nodded. "Totally. When Noah and I were trying, I probably tested a hundred times, squinting and thinking I could see a line and sending him pictures to see if he could see it too."

"Same, Seb is scared to open his phone now in case it's a picture of another pregnancy test."

Duchess cocked her head at Snow. "How long have you been trying?"

"Only a few months."

"Well, go get it so Charlie can pee on it."

Lotus shooed her away and Snow jumped up from the table and took off upstairs.

"Thanks for this. I've never really talked about this with anyone but Noah."

"I can't imagine that kind of loss. It does explain why you shot Noah though."

Charlie looked at Lotus who was sitting on the chair with her ankle tucked under her leg. "How so? Because I'm still not sure I understand what I was doing or why."

"Control. You couldn't control what happened to your son, but by shooting Noah and getting him out, you controlled the situation. It might sound crazy, but grief does some strange things to people."

"No, it's not crazy, and I think you're right. I'm just terrified I might go off the rails again and this pregnancy, if I am pregnant, is my biggest fear and a blessing at the same time. I don't know how to feel, to be honest."

"Have you ever spoken to someone about it?"

"Not really."

"I have a grief counsellor who helped me. I can give you her number."

"Thanks, Lotus, and you too, Duchess. I've never had this before and it's nice."

"No worries, we got you, Chica. Now go pee and let's find out."

Charlie took the test Snow was holding out and headed to the bathroom with the three women following.

"You gonna wait outside the door?"

Three heads nodded and she smiled because it felt good to have this support, to have friends. It had been a long time since she'd had that, if ever. A girl in high school for a few months before her mother had chased her off with her fucked up ways.

Doing her business she washed her hands and opened the door. "Well?"

"We have to wait."

"Uh, no we don't. There's no denying that line."

Charlie peered over Snow's shoulder and sure enough, a strong pink line was already clear in the test section. She was pregnant with her ex-husband's baby and had no idea if she wanted to cry or dance. "Looks like we're having a baby."

Duchess rested her hand on her shoulder and Charlie glanced at her, panic rising in her chest. Her vision went blurry as the world became a distant cloud of noise.

"She's gonna pass out. Lotus, grab her arm."

Charlie was marched to the couch in the airy living room and pushed into a seated position with her head between her legs. Snow sat beside her and counted her breathing with her until she felt like she wasn't going to faint.

Slowly lifting her head, she looked at her new friends and knew whatever happened she wasn't alone. "God, what is Noah going to say?"

"Bishop will be ecstatic. He adores you, any fool can see that. And that was before we saw you together. You're like one of those sappy romance novel couples Duchess reads. You're meant for each other and if he doesn't react as we want, we'll just kick his ass and set him straight."

"Thank you, guys. I wasn't expecting this."

"We got you, and until then, our lips are sealed." Duchess motioned zipping her lips and gave a warning glare to the other two who did the same.

Charlie laughed and felt lighter than she had this morning. She was pregnant but she'd figure it out.

CHAPTER 19

"We found them!" Bishop barrelled through the door of the rectory and found Charlie, Lotus, Snow, and Duchess in the living room laughing and eating chocolate truffles.

Charlie jumped to her feet and rushed to him as Duchess stood. "Tell me."

"The last building Reaper and I were watching was real quiet. But then we had Nkosi put in a call to the number and not long after, a van rolled out and it was the same one we caught on CCTV the night Andrea went missing."

They'd thought they'd caught a break when the van had been spotted as it traced back to the clinic. The CCTV had lost it in a dead zone and hadn't picked it back up. It was that which helped Watchdog narrow things down, though and get the building on the radar.

"The van picked up the woman from the clinic Titan and Hurricane were watching, and the same van just entered the building we were watching."

"Which building?"

Duchess was already laying blueprints over the coffee table.

He pointed at what looked like a country house or retirement home. "This one here."

"This is registered as a private residence but the ownership traces back to the clinic. Let me get Watchdog on the call with us."

"Shouldn't we let Bás know?" Lotus asked, hopping from foot to foot with barely suppressed energy. Of all the people in Shadow, she seemed to need the constant stimulation of the hunt the most.

"No, he's off the grid meeting with a team who might be able to help us in the US."

Bishop looked at Charlie and then Duchess. "We're expanding?"

"Not exactly but we're stretched too thin. We need more people as we evolve."

Bishop shrugged. He agreed but he was more interested in the now than asking questions about the future.

Watchdog popped up on the monitor Duchess had set on the table beside the couch.

"Morning, humans. Did you know Loch Ness might actually be a giant whale dick and not a monster at all?"

Reaper made a face of disgust. "Eww, gross, I did *not* need to know that."

"It's true, whales mate in groups of three, so the second male just hangs around with his wang out until it's his turn."

"As much as I want to discuss whale dicks, we have a possible location on the girls."

Watchdog sat closer to the screen. "Hit me." He was all business now as he waited for Duchess to give him the information he needed.

"The last property, Connolly Hall. We need to know how many people are inside and where. Along with anything to back up what Bish and Reaper saw."

"On it. Give me fifteen minutes."

Watchdog hung up and Bishop took a second to look at the

woman he loved, who was smiling and looking more relaxed than she had when he'd left. He'd been wary about leaving her alone with the girls. He loved them like sisters but they were a lot to handle. It seemed he'd been wrong to worry. An invisible bond had formed as they seemed to communicate without words like women did sometimes.

"So, you ladies have fun while we were out working hard?"

Charlie grinned and looked at her feet. "We bonded over a mutual love of chocolate and Chris Hemsworth."

"Urgh, first Lucía and now you lot. What is it with that perfectly muscled, grinning hunk of Australian flesh that you women can't get enough of?"

"Looks like you have a man crush, Reaper."

"Oh, please. I could take him any day."

"Oh, give me a chance and so could I." Duchess fanned herself and Charlie laughed.

Duchess cocked her head at Reaper. "Speaking of Lucía, how is our lovely princess?"

Reaper grinned and it was easy to see the adoration he had for the woman he loved. "She's great. She's with her mother and sister working on a charity ball for this winter."

Bishop was happy to see his friend so happy and even happier to see Charlie smiling with such ease. While he wasn't fond of her drooling over other men, he was happy to see the smile on her face. He hooked her around the waist and brought her to his side. "Looks like I have competition."

She turned her face toward him, his lips nearly touching hers. "Not even close."

His heart did a funny little twist at her words and the way she laid her head on his chest. This was right in every way. It was like being lost and suddenly finding the way home again.

The monitor lit up and Duchess answered the call from Watchdog. "What you got?"

"There are twenty-eight heat signatures inside the building.

Which is a lot, if it truly is a private residence but I don't think it is. A medical supply company delivers there three times a week, and from the inventory, it certainly suggests there are expectant mothers inside along with newborns."

"Fuckers," Bishop bit out, his grip tightening on Charlie who placed a hand over his abdomen, instantly calming the lava of anger in his belly.

"We're gonna need back up. We can't just go in guns blazing. They could kill the mothers or the babies, so we need to be smart about this."

Bishop's gut had him wanting to rush in, but he knew Duchess was right. They needed to be smart, too many innocents were at risk here. "I can put in a call to Jack and see if he can loan us some men."

"Good idea. See if Fortis can spare any too. Some will be the guards and I think the best plan is detailed surveillance on the property for twenty-four hours so we can learn the patterns of the security personnel. We also need to keep eyes on Carter, though I can probably get that dealt with so we won't have to worry about him."

"Speaking of Carter, I found something very interesting regarding him when I was poking around."

Bishop rolled his hand for Watchdog to get on with it. "And?"

"Marsha Cavendish has a link to Joel Hansen."

"Hansen? The one we've been hunting since he fucked over Jack's wife and sister-in-law?" Bishop asked wanting to clarify.

"Yes, it seems that Marsha was one of the first girls involved in Project Cradle. In those days the participants were voluntary. She signed up straight out of school, but she wasn't called Marsha then, she was Molly Mills."

"As in the Director of the CIA Mills?"

Watchdog pointed at the screen. "Got it in one. She's his daughter and got mixed up with a bad lot. He signed her up when she got pregnant by some nobody and then two years later she was reinvented as Marsha and went on to marry Winston Cavendish."

"We need to get this information to Bás."

"Already done."

"Do I want to know how you found what I'm assuming is extremely classified information?"

"You do not," Watchdog responded with a grin.

Duchess rolled her eyes. "Fine, can you coordinate from there or are you coming out of your lair?"

"My lair is where the magic happens, so I'll stay here."

"Okay. Talk later."

Charlie looked around the room. "Can someone catch me up?"

Bishop wasn't sure what he was allowed to tell her. Although she'd been allowed into the compound, the case details were private. Duchess gave a slight nod, and he was about to open his mouth when Reaper began to explain.

He let Charlie go as she moved to the couch and sat beside his friend while he explained the details to her. Bishop knew it was his way of making up for what he'd said and after a few days, things were back to normal between them. Hearing his doubts about Charlie had been hard, but now that there'd been time between the incident, he could acknowledge that he would've been the same way.

Slipping into the kitchen he grabbed a bottle of water for himself and a soda for Charlie.

"That for Charlie?"

Bishop glanced at Lotus who was tidying up some crumbs while they waited for Duchess to give them her orders. "Yes, why?"

"Give her the Fanta. It has less caffeine."

Bishop looked at the can of cola and then frowned before dismissing it as Lotus being Lotus. "Sure, why not."

Back in the room he took the seat on the other side of her and handed her the can, which she took with a smile for him as Reaper wrapped up the past.

"Wow, so Bás has a history with him. Jack and Lopez must want that asshole dead, and he's knee deep in this Project Cradle mess."

"That about sums it up, yes."

"And you've had no luck finding him?"

"No, he went dark after the incident with Lopez and Adeline."

"And Adeline was CIA and had Hansen's daughter. Which is how you found out about Cradle?"

"Yes. The only good thing the man did was walking away and leaving his daughter unharmed."

"Yeah, well, people will do a lot for their kids."

"I guess."

"Changing the subject slightly, what's happening with Nkosi?"

Charlie hated him but he knew she wanted to see him charged, not dead. Shadow handled a lot of kill orders for the boss lady but if they could have it dealt with without death, they would.

"He's being sent back to his own country where they'll deal with him."

"Ouch. They won't go easy on him."

"Nor should they."

Charlie sipped the can slowly, and he noticed she looked rosy-cheeked. "You okay?"

"Yeah, just a little tired. I was up early."

"Yeah, I heard you."

Reaper had made himself scarce and it was just the two of them. "Sorry I woke you."

Bishop leaned forward and brushed a thumb over her cheek. "You'd tell me if something was up, right?"

"Yes of course." She went to open her mouth again, but Duchess walked in.

"I have your orders."

Charlie jumped up and went to Duchess and he frowned, wondering if he was missing something then put it down to it all being new and yet old, and Charlie being slightly anxious with her sister still missing.

Getting up he crossed the room and waited for Duchess to give him his orders.

"Eidolon is sending five men and Fortis another five, so that's ten on top of our seven in the field and Watchdog on comms. Rykov is in Russia and still handling some business there but he should be back next month. For now, we have what we have, and it will have to be enough. Back up should be here by tonight but until then, I want full surveillance on the property from all angles."

Kneeling, she pointed at the plans spread out on the floor. "Snow, Reaper, I want you here, watching the back of the property. Hurricane and I will take the left side that backs onto the forest. Lotus and Titan, take the front from this position just off the road, and Bishop and Charlie on the right."

Bishop wasn't thrilled to be given the right side where most likely less would happen but he'd follow orders.

"That's it. Watchdog will handle internal surveillance by hacking the cameras inside and confirming what we think we know." Standing she glanced at Charlie. "We all good?"

"Yes, Duchess."

"Good, now get going and everyone stay on comms. I don't want anyone moving on this until backup arrives no matter what you witness. Do you copy?"

"Yes, boss."

"Crack on. I have to make a call first."

Bishop wrapped an arm around Charlie and kissed her head. "We're back, baby."

Her smile was radiant, and he wished he had a camera to capture it for all eternity. This felt right, working together, being together. It was like his life had suddenly righted itself.

Waiting for the call to go through, Duchess wondered if he'd help her after their last conversation. Things had become very complicated between her and Damon since he'd found her and Gideon flirting. It had only been one kiss, but Damon felt betrayed and rightly

142

so. They'd formed a friendship built on mutual respect and trust, and she'd lied to him about her attraction to his grumpy, growly brother.

"Yes?"

"Hi, it's me."

"I can read a damn phone screen, Nadia."

"Yeah, sorry. Listen I know I have no right to ask, but I need a favour."

"Go on?"

Damon was such a good man and she wished like hell her attraction was to him, not his asshole brother who'd made her turn into some simpering, submissive idiot when he was around. "I need you to keep Carter busy tomorrow night."

"No, absolutely not."

"Please, we have something, and I need to know he's busy so we can execute it without having to worry about him."

"Stop talking. I can't hear this shit. I'm a fucking barrister for Christ's sake."

"I know and I won't tell you any of the details but I really need your help, Damon."

Duchess could hear him sigh down the phone and imagined him pinching the bridge of his nose with impatience. "I'll try but I make no promises. Carter has been a little unstable the last few weeks. Do you know anything about that?"

"I might, but I can't tell you anything right now."

"We need an end game, Nadia. I can't keep this up much longer. I want this operation shut down and Gideon feels the same. He's getting in deeper and deeper. The shareholders are making things difficult and that bitch Marsha is bleeding our father dry, both financially and mentally."

"I know and I promise we're making progress. Hang in there, please?"

"When are you coming back?"

"Hopefully next week. Has Gideon fired anyone lately?"

Gideon was the boss from hell, demanding, rude, overly critical, and expected people to work day and night. She was just glad her cover was as a PA to Damon, she'd likely stab Gideon with a blunt spoon. God knew how he got away with it, but being a rich, handsome asshole seemed to have its perks.

"The latest girl lasted a day. The agency is threatening to blacklist him if he makes another personal assistant cry."

"Asshole."

"Yeah he is and yet you like that kind of thing."

"Can we not do this, Damon?"

"Fine, I just don't want you to get hurt."

"I know. You're a good friend."

"You know you're the first woman to friend-zone me in thirty-three years."

"It's good for your ego, and in any case, we'd kill each other."

"True. Now give me the details so I can try and help you."

Duchess told him what she'd need from him, and he said he'd try.

"You owe me."

"Fine."

"Good, I'm glad you agree. I have a gala to attend next Friday and need a date that won't annoy me all night."

"Do I need to cover my ink?"

"No, you're perfectly acceptable like you are."

"Then we have a deal."

"I'll text you with the details. Stay safe, Nadia."

"You too, Damon."

Duchess hung up and smiled. He was the first person outside of Shadow who she'd consider a friend. They'd spent the last year trying to get all the evidence they needed to take down Carter. Damon and Gideon agreeing to help had been a blessing. But to stop the business from collapsing to a degree it could destabilise the economy with job losses, they'd had to be careful. She hoped they were in the end game now with this news of Marsha and Carter's link to Cradle.

She sure hoped so, because every second she had to spend next to Gideon Cavendish she was closer to either murdering him in his sleep or jumping his delicious, annoying, growly bones.

CHAPTER 20

CHARLIE KNEW SHE HAD TO TELL NOAH ABOUT THE BABY. A BABY. SHE'D never thought she'd say those two words again, but here she was with a gift she hadn't known she needed. Terror was like a stealer of joy every time she tried to think of the future though.

At the moment, the house was full as the men from Eidolon and Fortis were brought up to speed on what they'd found from the last twenty-four hours of surveillance.

"You take the lead, Duchess."

Jack held his palm out for Duchess to take the lead on this mission. With so many big hitters in one room, it would be easy for egos to take over but both the leaders from Fortis and Eidolon were happy to cede the floor.

Eidolon had brought Jack, Gunner, Decker, Waggs, and Blake. They'd also arrived with Dr Decker, who was married to Mark Decker, Eidolon's profiler. She was a surgeon and having her there in case any of the women needed immediate medical attention had been a good call.

Fortis had arrived with Zack, the man who ran the show, Dane his second, Zin who she only knew by his reputation as the Viper,

Smithy, and last but not least Daniel, who bore a strong resemblance to the hot bearded guy from Magic Mike.

Jack had smiled when he'd seen her and Bishop together and she felt like she had his approval. She'd try and catch him after this was over so she could thank him for what he'd done for Noah.

"I propose we breach from three sides of the property around three am. It's when the place is the quietest, the guards will be tired, and the surprise attack gives us an advantage. I've arranged for Carter Cavendish to be occupied so we won't have to worry about him and the chatter is picking up nothing to suggest they know we're coming."

Rolling out the plans on the kitchen island, which was the only area big enough to fit them all, Duchess pointed at three dots on the plan. "These three positions are the weakest. If we breach in unison, we can cover the areas faster and decrease the likelihood of casualties. We know there are civilians inside and some will be doctors and possibly nurses, but we can't assume they're unarmed just because they have a white coat or are wearing a nurses' uniform."

Charlie listened as Duchess explained the plan in detail, stopping every now and again to consider options from either Jack or one of the other military operators who probably had more experience in the field than she did.

"You okay with this?"

Twisting she looked up at Noah and couldn't help the sliver of fear that wound its way inside her belly at the thought of something happening to him. "Yes, it's a solid plan."

"Not what I meant."

Her smile was small as she patted his cheek. "I know, but I'm trying to not let fear control me, so I'm ignoring it."

"Nobody would judge if you sat this out, Charl."

"I know, but that would be worse. I need to be there and make sure Andrea is okay."

Noah kissed her lips, the contact firm and innocent as kisses went but she still felt her body soften as if just his touch could melt her body and soul. He felt it and gripped her upper arms, a twitch of his lips making him appear younger.

"Hold that thought until we get back because I'm taking you to bed for a week and we're not leaving it except for food."

Charlie smiled against his mouth. "Sounds perfect."

"Grab your gear," Duchess shouted as everyone began to move, grabbing vests and protective gear as well as their preferred weapons. As she fitted the vest over her abdomen she wondered for a second if she should be going. She knew Noah would do his nut when he found out, but she hadn't lied when she'd said she needed to be there for Andrea. Who knew what state she'd be in when they found her, and she deserved to have her sister step up for her. Plus, Charlie hoped when she told Noah about her plans to retire from the job he'd forgive her.

"Charlie, you got a second?"

Seeing Duchess standing in the doorway she nodded and followed her out, not looking at Noah who was watching them with interest.

Duchess pulled her out the back door and checked they were alone before crossing her arms. "You sure about this?"

"Yes, I need to be there and I won't do anything stupid."

"You told Bishop yet?"

"No."

"Don't you think you should? This is his child too."

"I know and I was about to, but I'm concerned the news will distract him and we both know one tiny distraction in this job can cost you your life."

Duchess looked sympathetic but also like the leader she was as she assessed her. "You do exactly what your team leader tells you, and if I think for one second you're in danger, I'll bench you. Bishop is already going to kill me for letting you go into danger knowing the circumstances but if you die, I won't be far behind you."

"I won't take any unnecessary risks, but I'll do my job."

"Fair point." Duchess shook her head as she straightened Charlie's vest and fussed with her straps to tighten them. "I'm so going to regret this."

As she was walking off, Charlie stopped her. "Thank you, Duchess. I mean that. You've been a good friend."

Duchess rolled her eyes and threw an arm around her shoulder. "Jeez, stop with the emotions. Nobody's going to die tonight."

They were laughing as they re-entered the room and found the teams suited and booted and ready for action. Her gaze landed on Noah who looked drop-dead gorgeous in his tactical gear. To be fair, he looked that way no matter what he wore.

"You two good?"

"Yeah, she was just checking I was okay because this is Andrea."

"And are you?"

"Yeah, I'm fine. She has the best of the best coming to rescue her and once we get her home we'll deal with everything else as it comes up."

"I'm proud of you, Charl."

His words stuck in her chest. He was the only person to ever have said them to her. "Thanks."

"Let's roll out."

They were using five vehicles, three for the teams and two to transfer the women to hospitals. Jack had also managed to have private emergency vehicles on stand-by a few miles out from the property. They'd dump the SUVs one klick out and hoof it in closer so as not to draw attention or noise. From there they'd get into position on the three sides and wait. At exactly three am, Watchdog would take out the internal and external cameras and kill all the lights. Smithy would have taken out the backup generator and they'd infiltrate with Reaper, Jack, and Daniel taking out the lookout guards at the same time.

It was planned down to the finest detail but they all knew they couldn't plan for the unexpected which always happened. They just had to be aware and swivel if needed.

The vehicle she was in bumped over a pothole as they drove the fifty minutes across Leeds to the outskirts, each SUV taking a different route so a convoy wouldn't be obvious to anyone watching.

Duchess had kept the teams together with Eidolon as one, Fortis as two, and Shadow as three. It was a good call as far as she could tell because each team knew each other's moves and could anticipate a reaction from the person who had their back. She was the unknown and she wouldn't let them down. Not Noah, not Andrea, and not Duchess. She wouldn't let anyone get hurt because of her. The urge to lay her hand over her belly was strong but she resisted, not wanting to bring attention to it. Noah was far too astute and he already suspected something. He was too aware sometimes. Nausea swirled and she couldn't tell if it was nerves or morning sickness, which was clearly named by a man who'd never carried a baby, because it was any time of the day or night sickness.

"Chewy?"

Noah offered her some gum, and she grinned, knowing he'd noticed her nerves or perhaps the tinge of her skin. "Thanks."

The dip of his head and the way he rested his hand on her thigh was comforting and she had a good feeling that if they could get past this, they could make a real go of it this time. With some talking and some healing, perhaps the past could teach them enough to make the future shine.

The vehicle drew to a stop amongst the dense landscape of the countryside, the late summer vegetation working in their favour. Adjusting her vest and securing her weapon at her side, she started the trek to the property where she prayed her sister was safe. Noah's back in front of her and Hurricane behind her, she felt safe as she listened for the sounds of the night. An owl call, followed by a female fox scream made a shiver pass down her spine. Reaching the edge of the forest, Duchess held her fist up beside her head for them to halt. Hunkering down they waited, the comms checks had been done and now it was a waiting game before they got the go-ahead.

The team from Eidolon were taking the front, Fortis the service entrance, and Shadow would be handling the side where they'd pinpointed most of the girls.

Cameras inside had shown women, in different stages of pregnancy being held in what looked like ordinary wards, except these women were drugged to a point they were barely conscious. Andrea hadn't been identified, but Charlie was certain she was there. Some of the single rooms that showed heat signatures had no cameras inside, and that in itself was a thought Charlie didn't want to consider.

"Go in thirty."

The thirty-second warning had Charlie tensing and forcing any thoughts other than the mission out of her brain. A hand on her ankle made her glance at Noah who nodded his encouragement and she offered him a smile to reassure him she was okay.

"Go."

Reaper took out the guards closest to them as Jack and Daniel did the same.

"Clear to breach."

It was go-time as she fell into position between Noah and Hurricane. Keeping low, she shot the first man who ran around the corner completely unaware and he dropped to the ground. Stepping over him she heard the sounds of gunfire and blocked it out as she continued inside through the side door.

Inside, a large kitchen was to the left and a hallway in front. Noah motioned he was going to go ahead, and as a practised formation they spread out and began to clear the rooms. Sweeping the kitchen she almost missed the man crouched behind the large butcher block but caught his movement and spun just as he knocked the gun out of her hand.

Off balance, she dropped low as he threw himself at her and she rolled, feet in the air to block him from landing on her body. As they grappled she tried to reach her knife at her ankle but couldn't quite get her fingers to it.

As his fingers closed around her throat, she felt his body bow and then he went stiff, wide eyes looking at her in shock as his fingers went slack and he slumped against her. Kicking his inert body off her she saw Reaper holding a hand out to help her up.

"Thanks."

"Pleasure, Angel."

"Oh, please don't start with the Charlie's Angels references."

Reaper chuckled as he handed her weapon back to her and they continued up the back stairs from the kitchen to the second floor. Seeing Jack and Blake coming up the main stairs, she nodded.

"First floor is clear, proceeding to evacuation."

Zack's voice over the comms sounded calm as if this was a training exercise and she wondered how they kept so cool doing these kinds of extractions.

Touching the first door handle, she entered, her weapon steady as her light came over a woman lying in the bed, her belly huge and her eyes wide with panic.

"It's okay. I'm not here to hurt you. Can you walk?"

Frozen with terror the woman didn't respond until Charlie lowered her weapon and took her helmet off so the woman could see her face. "Can you walk?"

A nod was all she got but she'd take it. "Let's go." Placing an arm under the woman's armpit, she helped her toward the door where Jack took her and helped her down the stairs.

"Carry on clearing these rooms."

Charlie went from room to room, spotting glimpses of Noah doing the same.

He spotted her and frowned. "Get your helmet back on."

Charlie nodded and reached for it, only to realise she'd left it on the floor in the first room.

"Guys, hurry it up. We have incoming." Watchdog in her ear gave a warning.

"How long?" Duchess responded sounding annoyed.

"Six vehicles about five miles out."

"Fuck, wrap this up."

152

Moving quickly, Charlie ignored the lost helmet and concentrated on finding her sister. The code word would be said when she was located and so far nobody had seen her. Stress was making nausea roll through her belly and she pushed it down, ignoring it as she headed back out into the hallway.

The shock made her knees almost buckle as she saw Andrea standing in the hallway, a dazed look on her face, a thin pale nightgown covering her body. "Andrea."

She saw Noah rush toward her sister, calling her name and the familiar voice prompting Andrea to turn toward him. They were close to the top of the stairs across the hall from her. A flicker of movement to her left saw a man in scrubs exit a room and she watched in horror as he lifted his weapon to shoot the two people she loved the most. Firing her gun at the man, Charlie swore when nothing happened, the damn thing jammed. Her eyes flew to the man she loved.

"Noah!"

The man she loved was covering her sister with his body as she put her hands in the air and did the only thing she could and dove toward them. She felt the impact of the bullet tearing through her hand as Noah screamed her name, and then everything went black.

CHAPTER 21

"Nooo!"

He saw it happen in slow motion like his worst nightmare as he dropped his arms from Andrea and ran to Charlie as she hit the floor. Reaper had ended the doctor who'd shot at them, but right now all he could think about was Charlie.

Skidding to his knees he looked at her limp body, and with shaky hands reached for her hand which was a bloody mess.

"Out of the way."

Bishop heard Waggs as the Eidolon member fell to his knees beside him and started checking Charlie over. Removing the hand covering her face, Bishop groaned seeing the bullet had struck her in the head.

"I've got a pulse, but we need to move her fast." Waggs looked up then. "Jack, call Savannah and have her meet me out the back."

Bishop didn't know what to do, so he held her uninjured hand and prayed and begged her not to die. "Don't you dare die on me, Charlie. I need you to live so we can make that future we dreamed about."

His hand remained in hers as Waggs and Reaper and the others worked to keep her alive.

"Charlie?"

The small voice at his side had him glancing at Andrea who looked terrified and confused, her hair a wild, matted mess, and she had bruises on her wrists and face. Charlie had been trying to save them and he knew it was his duty to keep Andrea safe until Charlie came back to them.

"Andrea, it's me, Noah." He opened his arm for her, not daring to let go of his wife. Dragging her gaze from her sister she looked at him and seemed to crumple as she ran to him and buried her face in his chest, sobs erupting from her chest.

Shouts and hurried words surrounded them as Charlie was loaded onto a gurney and Waggs barked urgent orders at people and he prayed to anyone he could think of for his Charlie to live.

"It'll be okay, Andrea. She's a fighter."

Letting go of her, he passed her off to Lotus who wrapped a blanket around his sister-in-law's shoulders and led her down the stairs.

"Hurry the fuck up, we're losing her."

Bile burned his throat as they reached the bottom of the stairs, Charlie still limp and unresponsive, an IV in her arm, electrodes on her chest.

Savannah Decker came rushing through the cleared hallway with a rucksack on her back.

"Head wound, breathing but tachycardic. BP eighty-five over forty."

"We need to intubate. She isn't protecting her airway."

Bishop went to run his hands through his hair and realised he hadn't even taken his helmet off. Ripping it from his head, he cursed himself for not forcing Charlie to put her's back on.

Savannah was forcing a tube down her throat to connect an airway as Waggs began CPR.

Falling to his knees, he couldn't stop the tears that poured unchecked down his face. He was losing her again, only this time it would be permanent. A life without her was unthinkable. She was his everything, his soulmate. He saw Lotus whisper to Savannah who nodded before continuing what she was doing.

"Please don't let her die. Please, God, don't take her from me."

"Bishop?" Duchess laid her arm gently around his shoulders. "They're Life Flighting her to the nearest trauma hospital. Do you want to go with them?"

"Yes."

He swiped his fist across his wet eyes and jumped as Waggs shouted they had a pulse. Relief made his belly bottom out and he wasn't sure his legs would hold him, but Reaper came up behind him and took his weight as he helped him out to the chopper which was on the tarmac drive. Loading her inside he could hardly see her with the tubes and bandages that covered her. Savannah jumped up beside her as Waggs gave the paramedics all the relevant details before stepping back to allow him entry. Hauling himself up, he took a seat and prayed the entire flight that she wouldn't die, that their story wasn't over.

As they landed a few short minutes later, Charlie was rushed into the resuscitation area and he was blocked by a nurse with a hand on his chest.

"You can't go in there."

"I need to be with her. I'm her husband."

A sympathetic expression moved over her face. "Let the doctors do their jobs. You can wait in the family room, and someone will come and get some details from you shortly. Dr Decker is the best. You're incredibly lucky to have her with you. If anyone can save your wife, it's her."

As she disappeared into the room, he caught a glimpse of his wife surrounded by doctors and nurses, all of them working to keep her alive.

Moving to the door of the family room he sank down the wall, his legs no longer strong enough to hold him as he replayed the incident over and over again in his head.

"Bishop."

Lifting his heavy head, he saw Reaper, Snow, Hurricane, Titan, and Duchess walking toward him. They were all decked out in tactical gear, their faces a stony mask as they moved toward him.

"I'm not leaving." He knew they were exposed, and it could blow everything they'd worked for at Shadow being at the hospital, but he wouldn't leave her.

"Nobody is asking you to leave. Jack is handling everything."

"Jack is here?"

Reaper reached down for his arm and pulled him to his feet so they could guide him into the private room that had seemed too far away just seconds ago.

"Eidolon had us flown here, and they're handling the clean-up at the site."

"Andrea, is she...?" His hand shook as he scrubbed it down his face and he clenched his fist to try and stop the motion.

"Lotus is with her, and she's being seen by a doctor. I told her we'd keep her informed."

Hanging his head in his hand between his knees, he wished like hell he'd made Charlie stay home.

"Don't do that, Bishop, don't second guess yourself. Charlie wouldn't have stayed home if you'd asked."

He glanced up to see his teammates all surround him in chairs around the small room. "Why did she take her damn helmet off?"

Reaper lifted his head and Bishop saw haunted eyes meet his. "The first girl she found was frozen with fear, she wouldn't move and was heavily pregnant. Charlie took her helmet off to show her she was one of the good guys."

"Typical Charlie." His words held resignation and a touch of anger. "She should never have put herself between me and a bullet."

"She loves you, Bish."

"I know, and God, I love her so much I can't breathe without her."

A hand landed on his shoulder, and he saw Hurricane beside him. "She's a fighter, Bish. She's strong and you give her a reason to fight this."

Bishop didn't know what to say to that. She was a fighter but a bullet in the head was about as bad as it got. They'd need a miracle to bring her out of this and even then, would she even know him or have any kind of physical or mental capacity? The damage could be catastrophic, and Charlie wouldn't want that.

The door opened and Savannah walked in wearing scrubs.

"Savannah?"

He jumped to his feet and met her halfway as she took his hands in hers and looked him in the eye with a steady, determined stare. "Noah, we're taking Charlie into surgery now. I'm going to operate to remove the bullet from the front of her right temporal lobe. The bullet passed through her hand first so I'm hoping that the high velocity and lack of wobble on the bullet has helped us, but I won't lie. This is bad, and it's going to be a long, complex surgery, but I'll do everything in my power to bring her back to you. However, I can't make any promises about the baby. Charlie had a lot of blood loss, but so far the pregnancy, though very early, is intact."

"Baby?" Bishop felt like he'd been sucker punched in the gut, the room seemed to tunnel around him, the air got stuck in his lungs as he tried to force it out and everything felt fuzzy.

Savannah squeezed his hands. "Noah, focus on me." He did and the air exploded from his lungs as he followed her deep breaths in and out. "I take it you were unaware."

"I was. I mean I didn't know."

"Well, as I said it's very early. I'll send a nurse out with updates when I can."

"Thank you."

Savannah nodded and turned on her heel to go save the most important people in his world.

Sinking to the soft chair he fell back, his brain and body struggling to process it all. Charlie was pregnant and she'd thrown herself in front of a bullet. "What the fuck was she thinking?"

Anger was the only emotion he felt as he stood abruptly and shoved his way past his friends.

"Where are you going?"

He waved Titan off. "I need air."

He was suffocating, that's how he felt. Like he couldn't breathe, like he was dying. Reaching the exit he stumbled through and dropped his hands to his knees and sucked in air. Pregnant, she was having his baby and now she might die, and he'd lose them both. This was a nightmare and he couldn't seem to wake up.

"Bishop?"

He growled not wanting to deal with anyone right now. "Go away, Snow."

"She loves you and she loves this baby."

Standing, he felt the first stab of suspicion as his glare landed on Snow. "You knew?"

Her eyes met his before dropping to the floor. "She was sick earlier today, so we got her to take a test. She was going to tell you as soon as you got home, but then we found the location and it all happened so fast."

He advanced on Snow. "She was pregnant, and you let her go into the building and put herself in danger! How could you?"

"I...." Tears hit Snow's eyes, but he felt no sympathy for her.

"Don't take it out on her, it was my call."

Looking beyond Snow, he snorted in disgust at Duchess, who had her arms folded across her chest. "Some call to send her out there when she'd just had this news. Do you know how big of a deal it would be for her to find out she was unexpectedly pregnant after everything we went through?"

"Of course I do. I spoke with her before we left and asked if she was okay. She said she needed this."

Bishop clicked his tongue. "Of course she fucking said that.

Charlie would never stand down when people she cares about are in danger." He pointed a finger at Duchess. "That was your fucking job, and you blew it. If she dies it's your fucking fault and I'll never forgive you."

"That's enough. Take a fucking walk, Bishop."

Bishop rounded on Jack who'd appeared from nowhere and clenched his teeth, the urge to lash out and hurt someone almost more than he could bear. "Fuck this and fuck you."

Bishop stormed off, not having any clue where he was going to go, just needing to remove himself before he did something he might regret.

Hours later he was sitting outside on the bench as cars began to fill the carpark with shift changes and patients arrived for early appointments. The tranquillity of the children's memorial garden had calmed him some.

"Thought I might find you here."

Hurricane sat down beside him, and he looked at the floor, too frightened to ask for an update on his wife in case he was given news he couldn't handle. Fuck, she wasn't even his wife now, not legally at least.

"Nurse came out, said it was going as expected and Charlie was holding her own."

His belly flopped and he thought he might faint from relief, even if it was only temporary.

"Thanks."

"I won't ask how you're doing because I can't even imagine what you're going through, but I do know it wasn't Duchess' fault."

Bishop side-eyed his friend. "You heard?"

"Yeah, Snow was pretty upset."

"I'll apologise."

"They get it, man. They understand how hard this is for you or at least they're trying."

"She should never have been there."

"Maybe, but it was her call to make. Would you have been able to stop her?"

He'd been considering that for the last few hours and decided Charlie would've done what she thought was best. Her determination was one of the things he loved about her. "I don't know, maybe. Probably not."

"Seems to me instead of hating our girls for keeping her secret, you should be happy Charlie had women ready to keep her secrets and surround her with what she needed when she needed it."

"Yeah?"

"Strikes me she isn't someone who opens up to many and yet she did to the girls. That's a good thing, surely?"

"Yes, it is. I just wish she hadn't got hurt."

A big palm landed on his back. "I know and I know the what ifs will be driving you crazy, but you can't live life like that, man."

Bishop sat up, wiping the dried blood on his hands over his trousers. "Speaking from experience?"

"Something like that."

"You're a closed book, Hurricane."

His friend shook his head. "Nah, but this ain't the time for my story."

"Fair enough."

"Now, why don't you get washed up and come back inside? Andrea is waiting for you with the others."

"They're still here?"

"We're family, man. Where else would we be?"

"Thanks, Warren."

A grin spread over his friend's face. "Come now, man, this ain't the time to break out the first names."

"Fine, Hurricane. Let's go and start my apology tour."

He didn't have all the answers or even a plan past the next few minutes, but he knew falling out with the people who'd picked him up and shown him what family was when he was lost wasn't the answer.

CHAPTER 22

Bishop hated himself after walking into the room and seeing Duchess looking so broken. Her eyes moved over him, and he opened his arms as she jumped up and rushed into them.

"I'm so sorry, Bish."

Hugging her tight he stroked her hair. "No, I'm sorry. I was a knob and you didn't deserve that. Thank you for being with Charlie when she found out."

Pulling back, he saw her blink away the wetness in her eyes, her strong outer core falling into place.

"It wasn't just me. Lotus and Snow were there, too. Charlie is the best."

He took in Snow and Lotus who looked worried sick, their expressions pinched with guilt. "Thank you, all of you. I couldn't get through this without you guys."

Reaper and Titan were seated by Jack and Mark Decker, who'd appeared as well as Blake, Waggs, Gunner, Zack, Smithy, Zin, Dane, and Daniel. All of them were in the room, which was unheard of because one of their own had been hurt.

Emotion choked his throat as his eyes came to rest on Andrea who was asleep with her head on Titan's shoulder. He moved to crouch beside her and Lotus. "She okay?"

"Yes, a few bruises and scrapes but she'll recover. Physically at least."

"The baby?" He could hardly get the words out without them clogging his throat as he mentally shut that thought down, not allowing any hope into his heart right now.

"She miscarried a few days ago."

"Poor kid."

He stroked her hair and Lotus moved over so he could sit beside his sister-in-law. She didn't look like Charlie, but they had similar traits in the way they'd flick their heads or laugh.

His head leaning back against the couch, he looked at the ceiling as the murmured voices of his family moved around him. He should ask about the case and the others but he didn't have anything left in him. Just enough to pray and beg for the life of the woman he loved.

When the door opened he almost sprung from the seat like a jack in the box. "Savannah?" She looked exhausted, as she pulled the skull cap off her head. "How is she?"

"She did extremely well. We managed to remove the bullet from the lateral sulcus and it appears as if minimal damage was done to the brain itself. We won't know for sure until she wakes up if there's any impairment or lasting damage of any kind. Her hand won't be winning any TV commercials but she should regain full use after physical therapy. She has a long road to recovery ahead and because of a slight herniation, she'll be kept in a medically induced coma to allow healing for a few days. All in all, it's the best outcome we could hope for so far."

"The baby?"

"We did a transvaginal scan, and the sac is intact but it's too early for a heartbeat, so we'll have to wait but from what we can see, it looks like a normal healthy pregnancy of this gestation."

"Thank you, Savannah. I don't know how I can thank you."

Savannah squeezed his hand. "You don't have to thank me. This is my job."

"It's more than that. You're a wonder, my darling."

Bishop moved aside as Mark wrapped his wife in his arms and kissed her head. Mark might be biased but he wasn't wrong, and he'd be eternally grateful she'd been the one there to save his wife when she needed it.

"Can I see her?"

"They're taking her up to the ICU and once she's settled you can go and see her. But might I suggest a quick shower first before you scare the staff?"

Bishop looked down at himself and the blood covering his clothes and blanched knowing it was Charlie's. "Yeah. Good plan."

Twenty minutes later, showered and clean, he was led toward the ICU where Charlie was being cared for. He hesitated outside, fearful of going in and seeing her, but he pushed through. His knees almost buckled, but he locked his knees and forced himself inside.

She was lying in a big bed with IVs in her arm, monitors strapped to her chest, and a drain wrapped bandage over her head. Her skin was pale, almost grey but as he glanced at the monitor he saw her BP and pulse looked good.

Taking her hand he sat beside her and hated how cold she was, her fingers on her uninjured hand cool to touch. "Hey, baby, it's me, Noah. I'm not sure if you can hear me, but I love you and I need you to know that the baby is fine. A baby, Charl. That's some secret you kept, but then I guess it wasn't for long."

He fell silent as the nurses came and checked on her, doing fifteen-minute observations.

"Talk to her. It's good for them to hear you."

Bishop glanced up to see a slim nurse with short curly hair smiling kindly at him as she adjusted Charlie's IV.

He sat like that all day, not leaving her side as he talked and told her of all the things he wanted to do with her, how much he loved her, and how much trouble she was in for risking her life for him.

As the day wore on, his friends brought food which he dismissed but the coffee was welcome. Around six pm Andrea poked her head in, and he beckoned her forward.

Warily she walked toward him, her hands in constant nervous movement.

"Hey, sis."

"Hi, Noah."

She looked nervous and he wasn't sure if that was from the trauma she'd been through or fear. "Here, sit." He dragged a chair up beside his and motioned her to sit noting how thin she was.

"Is she going to be okay?" She sounded every one of her twenty-one years as her small voice asked the question.

"I hope so. I believe if anyone can get shot in the noggin and make it, it's our Charlie."

A sob tore his gaze from his wife's gently moving chest.

Andrea seemed to mentally collapse in front of him.

"Hey."

"This is all my fault."

Wrapping his arm around her he pulled her head to his chest. "No, this isn't your fault. You did the right thing reaching out to Charlie. She loves you and she's your big sister."

"But if I hadn't got involved with Carter, this wouldn't have happened."

"Maybe but if you hadn't done that and reached out to Charlie, all those women would still be prisoners. You helped save them, Andrea."

She cried harder and he held her for a beat. "Talk to Charlie, let her know you're okay. She was so worried about you. She loves you so much."

Sniffing loudly, Andrea wiped her tears on the sleeve of her blue top, looking so young. He wanted to round up every fucker who was involved in this and annihilate them.

. . .

THE NEXT SEVERAL days were a constant stream of revolving people keeping him fed and caffeinated. Several nagged him to go to the safe house and shower or sleep, but he wouldn't leave her. Andrea came in and sat with him a few hours each day, but she was healing too, and he knew from Lotus she was getting help from a therapist to deal with her trauma.

Eidolon and Fortis had gone home but they'd handled the clean-up and the nursery, as one of the doctors arrested on site had called it.

"Hey."

Bishop turned to see Watchdog walking toward him. "Watchdog, what are you doing out of your lair?"

"Couldn't let my new trivia partner think I didn't care or visit." Bishop accepted his hug as he sat down next to Bishop's chair. "How's she doing?"

His eyes swept over Charlie. "Doc says she's doing well, her brain is healing, and her body is doing what it's meant to do. I just..."

"Want to see her wake up."

"Yeah, I need to see she's okay and find out what kind of recovery we're facing."

"Whatever it is, we're all here for you, Bish."

"They're going to wean her off the sedation later, so we'll see if she wakes up soon after."

"It can take up to a week to come out of an induced coma once they wean you off the drugs."

"Thanks, brains, is that from a book?"

"Nah, my mum had a car accident years ago and went through something similar."

Bishop felt awful. "Man, I'm so sorry. I had no idea."

"It's fine. She came through it okay."

"And she's fine now?" Watchdog didn't talk about his family except to say his mum had been his biggest cheerleader growing up and supported him fully.

"Physically she is."

Bishop didn't push for any more information but sensed there was way more to that story.

"Anyway, I'm here because you need a shower. The nurses are complaining and your stubborn ass won't listen to anyone. Get yourself back to the house, shower, sleep, eat, and then come back. I'm going to sit with my friend here and fill her with interesting facts for when we team up for the pub quiz."

"I..." He didn't get to finish before the door opened and Reaper stood there with Bás, who'd flown back to the UK the previous night.

"No arguments. Move your ass."

He glanced at Charlie and then Bás, torn on what to do. "Fine, but any slight change you call me."

"If she so much as moves a fingernail, I'll be on the blower."

"Okay. Thanks, Watchdog."

Bás drove him back as Reaper stayed with Watchdog outside the door to the ICU like a silent guard. Carter Cavendish was still out there, and the attack on the nursery had got him in a flap.

"Any news on Project Cradle?"

Bás pursed his lips. "Yeah, some. We found a definite link between Carter and Cradle. Seems he's been funding a lot of the UK operation. That was the main centre for the women before birth but we haven't found the mothers post-birth or the babies. We understand from some of the doctors and nurses arrested that they're taken straight after delivery to another location. Each stage of the process is kept separate from the next, so if something were to happen it wouldn't compromise the rest."

"So they're just going to set up somewhere else and start again."

Bás looked grim. "We're onto them now though and we know more than we ever have."

Bishop glanced at his watch already anxious to be back with Charlie. He sent Watchdog a text for an update.

BISHOP: HOW IS SHE?

WATCHDOG: THAT TOOK LONGER THAN I EXPECTED. SHE'S THE SAME ONLY NOW SHE'S AN EXPERT ON THE HISTORY OF THE SPANISH ARMADA.

Bishop rolled his eyes, but his lips twitched. Tucking his phone away he looked back at Bás. "So what now?"

"Well, Duchess has gone back under cover to try and get to Carter. She's taken this hard and is determined to end it."

Bishop laid his head back against the rest. "I was a dick to her."

Bás raised an eyebrow and frowned with the other. "Yeah, I heard."

"I did apologise."

Bás sighed. "Forget it, Bishop. We all know you didn't mean it, but Duchess holds herself to high standards and she feels she let you down. It's our job now to prove to her she didn't."

"How?"

"We catch these bastards and shut this nightmare down for good."

"And how, oh wise one, are we going to do that?"

"By bringing in backup."

"Who? Eidolon? Fortis?"

Bás shook his head. "No."

"Well, are you going to share?"

"Do you remember the SEAL Team who helped Adeline get away from Ravelino?"

"Yeah, they relocated her to Alaska."

"Yeah, well, they retired."

"Did they indeed?"

"Officially they did, but unofficially they didn't. They're going to work with us to look into the US side of this operation."

"Are we sure there is one?"

"Yes, that's what Valentina and I went to find out and they have a similar set-up to the UK, and that's not all. They have one in Europe too."

"Jesus, that's gonna need some sort of money to back it."

"Yeah and we start with Carter Cavendish and his evil mother or at least Duchess does, and we work behind the scenes to back her up."

"So this isn't going to be over for a while?"

"No. It's going to be slow, but we work smart."

"I'll need to be with Charlie some as I don't know what the future holds."

"We set up a property in the village for you both and Savannah is going to check on her when she goes home."

"If she goes home." A punch in the arm had him jumping back. "What the fuck?"

"Cut that negative shit out. Charlie is going to be fine, and we're going to fix this shit."

"When did you become Mr Sunshine and Roses?"

"When the alternative became unacceptable." The car stopped outside the rectory and Bás turned to him. "We're gonna fix this, Bishop, and then you can have your happy ending."

"I hope so, Bás. I hope so."

"Now get the fuck out of my car. I have work to do, and that doesn't include being your fucking chauffeur."

Bishop laughed but exited the car and headed inside, where Hurricane was waiting with a plate full of bacon, eggs, hash browns, beans, mushrooms, and tomatoes.

"Eat then shower. You fucking stink."

Bishop grinned as he accepted the plate and fell on the food like a starving man.

"You need to take better care of yourself. You're no good to Charlie if you're exhausted."

"Thanks, Mum."

Hurricane shot him the middle finger and wandered back to the coffee pot and poured him a coffee. "Once you've had some sleep I'll drive you back to the hospital." He took the plate away and walked back to the sink.

"Where is everyone else?"

"Lotus and Titan are showing Andrea some basic self-defence moves."

Bishop went to stand. "Is she ready for that?"

"She needs it, Bish. She's frightened and giving her the tools to feel safe is what she needs more than rest."

"What about Snow and Bein?"

"They headed back to Hereford to collate what we know and debrief with Eidolon and Fortis."

"I feel like I'm letting you all down."

Hurricane frowned and he looked pissed. "Don't make me hurt you, dickwad. You're where you need to be so cut that shit out right now."

"I know. I just feel helpless and useless."

"There'll be plenty of time for you to help out when Charlie wakes up."

"I guess you're right."

"Of course I am. Now shower before we have to have the property fumigated."

Bishop chuckled as he headed to the bedroom he'd last shared with Charlie a few days ago. Her scent clung to the sheets, and he sniffed like a freak before he headed for the shower, sleep, and then back to his wife.

CHAPTER 23

IMAGES AND SOUNDS SEEPED INTO HER CONSCIOUSNESS. BRIGHT LIGHTS AND the darkness of an empty hallway. Cries and loud urgent words were begging her for something, but she couldn't grasp what they wanted. A soft hand on her face, a flicker of awareness, and then nothing, blessed nothing.

Sounds were clearer now, her sister's voice so clear it sounded like she was whispering in her ear. But that wasn't right, her sister was lost, missing. Confusion battled with the terror that clawed at her chest. Noah, a man with a gun pointed at him, and then pain like nothing she'd ever felt before exploding in her head. Charlie fought to open her eyes to see, to find him in the thick fog of her mind but it was an impossible feat, and she fell back into an exhausted sleep.

A gasp for air had her eyes fluttering open and then closing quickly against the brightness of the light. Her limbs felt heavy and tired, her thoughts jumbled and confused as she tried to figure out what had happened.

"Charlie, baby, can you hear me?"

Opening her mouth she tried to respond to Noah's whispered request and failed, the cotton drying out every last ounce of moisture until speech felt impossible. A damp, cool cloth was placed against her lips, and she struggled to find the energy to wet them.

"Here."

A straw was held to her mouth, and she opened it on reflex as she sucked down the cool water. The pain in her sore throat instantly easing as she forced her brain to open her eyes again. This time the light was blocked by the face of the man she loved—her Noah.

"Noah?"

"Yes, baby, I'm here."

Lifting her hand that seemed to weigh a tonne she stroked at the tears coursing down his handsome face. "What happened?" Her voice was so hoarse she hardly recognised it as her own.

"Can you remember anything?"

Charlie felt her head begin to pound as memories began to pierce the fog of her brain. "I.. I... Andrea?"

"Andrea is fine. She's resting and Lotus is keeping a really good eye on her."

"Was I hurt?"

Noah looked down and away from her before lifting tear-filled eyes back up to her. "You were shot, Charlie. The bullet went through your hand and into your brain."

"I was?" She didn't know why she was asking that, Noah would never lie to her.

"Scared the fucking life out of me."

Her fingers grazed the stubble on his face, and she noticed the shadows under his eyes. "Sorry."

His lips grazed her fingertips and he shook his head. "You don't have a damn thing to be sorry about, baby."

Baby. Why did that word trigger such a visceral sense of fear and hope inside her?

"Hey, what's wrong? Let me call a doctor."

Charlie held on to his hand as he went to move and Noah looked back at her with sympathy.

"It's okay, I'm not leaving you. I'm never leaving you again,

172

Charl. I just want to press the buzzer." True to his word, Noah pressed the buzzer and sat beside her.

A nurse bustled in, her curly brown hair bouncy, her pretty smile filled with happiness. "Well aren't you a sight for sore eyes. Let me just do a few checks and the doctor will be in to see you." The nurse checked her monitors and temperature before nodding. "Looks good. How are your pain levels?"

Charlie wasn't sure, she kind of felt numb and disjointed like she didn't really know what was happening like this was a show and she was watching. "Okay, I guess."

"Well, we want to keep on top of it, so once the doctor has seen you, I'll be back."

Turning her head, slowly she saw Noah watching her as if she might disappear at any second. "How long have I been here?"

"All told, ten days. After you were shot you were placed in an induced coma, and they weaned you off the drugs about three days ago."

"Have you left at all?"

Noah smirked but it felt forced. "Do l look that bad?"

"Like roadkill."

Her touch of humour made him smile and this time it reached his eyes. "I love you, too."

Tears stung her eyes at his words. She would've given anything to hear them and maybe almost getting ghosted was worth it. "I love you more."

"Impossible."

"Ah, look who's awake."

Charlie dragged her gaze away from Noah to see a beautiful woman walking towards her rubbing alcohol gel on her hands. "Dr Decker?"

"I see I don't need to ask you what year it is, but let's go through a few questions anyway, okay?"

Charlie nodded and then wished she hadn't when her brain seemed to bounce around her head like a pinball with nails attached. Wincing, she squeezed Noah's hand and he kissed her knuckles.

"Yeah, maybe refrain from moving your head too quickly as well. You've been through quite a trauma and it will take some time."

Dr Decker proceeded to go through a bunch of questions as she checked Charlie's reflexes and reactions. It was exhausting and felt like being given a shock exam you were desperate to pass with no clue as to the content of the paper.

"Well, everything looks good, and it seems you're extremely lucky and should make a full recovery. It won't happen overnight and you'll need to rest and be patient, but I see no reason why you won't be back to kicking asses and taking names very soon."

Dr Decker cast a glance at Noah before turning back to her. "Is there anything you'd like to ask me?"

Charlie hated feeling so confused and groggy. "I can't remember everything. There seem to be gaps in my memory."

"Short- or long-term memory can be affected by a head injury of this magnitude. Do you remember Noah?"

His fingers brushed her arm and she felt safe, but she wasn't sure if they'd fixed what was broken between them or if this was a reaction to her getting hurt. "Yes, I remember everything up until we left Longtown."

"Short-term memory loss and especially around the incident where you were hurt is normal and should come back to you in a few days or weeks. Just be patient."

"Can't Noah tell me?"

"He can but I don't want you to rush this. It's better if you let things come back to you in increments. Forcing your brain to remember can be painful and frustrating."

"Okay." Charlie didn't like the idea that others knew what had happened and she didn't, but she was too tired to argue.

"I'll let you get some rest and come back later. Perhaps this one will leave for his second shower in ten days now you're awake."

Charlie felt her lips tip into a smile even as her eyes fought to stay open. The door closed behind the doctor who'd saved her life and Charlie let sleep take her, safe in the knowledge she was safe while Noah watched over her. That was how he'd always made her feel—safe, cared for, worth the trouble.

When she opened her eyes again it was to see her sister and Noah chatting in the corner of the large room. The seats, more like armchairs, faced the drizzle of rain outside the window. "Hey."

Noah grinned as he jumped up and rushed to her side, offering her some water for her parched throat. "How are you feeling?"

Charlie tested out her body for pain and found just the twinge in her hand and head, but otherwise a little better than the first time.

"Charlie."

Her sister looked lost and vulnerable, as she crossed her arms over her middle as if to protect herself. "Andrea." Charlie reached for her, and Andrea rushed to her, burying her head in Charlie's chest as she sobbed. Charlie placed her uninjured hand over her sister's head and let her cry as she cast a glance at Noah, who looked on with sadness and relief.

"How about I see if we can rustle up some soup while you two catch up?"

"Thank you."

Noah dropped a light kiss on her forehead before backing out of the room. An emptiness in her gut had her wanting to call him back, fear that he'd leave her an ache she couldn't pinpoint the reason for.

Andrea looked up through watery eyes, the once bright green a muted muddy colour now. "I'm so sorry."

"Hey, no you don't. You did nothing wrong."

"I should have known he was bad news."

Carter Cavendish, the man who had got her sister pregnant and then kidnapped her to be part of his fucked-up baby farm. She remembered that with clarity, so why not the days leading up to the shooting? "No, you shouldn't. He was probably charming and sweet and told you everything you wanted to hear until he had you where he wanted you."

"I still feel foolish."

"I know but you'll get through it."

Charlie wanted to ask about the baby and again the word sent pain spiralling through her head.

"You okay?"

"Yeah just adjusting." She'd never say she was in pain because they'd try and force more medication on her and she hated feeling so out of it.

Andrea looked down at her hands as she sat back in the chair. "I, um, lost the baby."

"Oh, Andrea, I'm so sorry."

"Is it awful that I felt relieved?"

"No, of course not. It was a big decision and held a lot of extra consideration with who the father was. Anyone would've been overwhelmed and having that choice taken away would be a relief in some ways."

"I just feel like I'm glad my baby died and that's not it. I just... I don't know how to feel."

"You feel however you want to and don't let anyone tell you what that is. You went through a huge trauma, and it will take a while and talking to an expert for you to come through this."

"That's what Lotus said."

A memory of Lotus handing her a buttered crumpet flew threw her mind and nausea raced up her throat. "She did?"

Her voice was weak as she forced the words out while trying to deal with the memories that were now flooding her brain like an avalanche. Snow and Lotus with Duchess, her eating a crumpet, nausea, sickness, a pregnancy test, and then the two pink lines. Noah, striding toward her with a smile on his handsome face. A look of love passed from him to her as he told her wanted a future with her again. Her son, his perfect face so sweet, so innocent, and Andrea and Noah, looking at her as a man raised his gun and then pain. So much pain tearing through her as Noah cried out for her, but she couldn't reach him. Her words stuck inside her head as he begged her to live.

"Charlie? Charlie? Baby, are you okay?"

Words came at her from a distance suddenly penetrating the cloud of memories. The room was now empty apart from her and Noah. His worried, beloved face was close as she glanced at him and knew she had to ask a question she wasn't sure she'd survive the answer to. "Our baby?" Her voice clogged with emotion, she held on as he wrapped her in his embrace. She wanted time to stand still so she could have that hope without having to deal with the fear she'd felt when she saw the positive test.

"Everything is fine. Savannah has checked twice, and our baby looks to be just fine."

Relief almost crushed her as she physically sagged in his arms and cried.

"It's okay, baby. I'm here and I'm not leaving you."

She cried harder at his words because she wasn't sure she could do it again. Risk the heartbreak of carrying their child who she loved already and things going wrong again. She wasn't strong enough, and worse, what if she hurt Noah again? What if she was broken and she couldn't carry a child? Yet this tiny child had survived being shot, had come to life through love, even if at the time it hadn't seemed that way. She was pinned between hope and terror and didn't know which way to turn.

CHAPTER 24

Bishop had thought seeing her unconscious and fighting for life was bad enough but the sheer terror in her eyes almost slayed him. Gripping her hand, he smoothed his thumb over her knuckles trying to calm her frayed nerves or maybe it was the pounding in his own heart he was trying to steady. "Talk to me. Tell me what's going through that pretty head of yours."

Charlie shook her head and he wanted to push but he had to remember she was only a few hours out of her coma and dealing with a lot. He had to rein in his own needs right now and let her lead her recovery.

Instead, he got up on the bed, knowing it would earn him a telling off from Natalie, the nurse who'd undertaken most of Charlie's care. Wrapping her in his arms, he held her while she cried quietly until she fell asleep.

He stayed that way, just holding her and wanting desperately to race to the end of their story and see how it ended for them and knowing wishes like that served no purpose.

The door squeaked open, and Savannah Decker poked her head inside. "Everything okay?"

He beckoned her inside and she glanced at the monitors, cataloguing every number until she was satisfied before taking the seat he'd vacated.

"She remembered the baby."

"Oh."

"Yeah, she freaked out. I didn't know what to do so I just held her until she fell asleep."

Savannah nodded. "That was the best thing to do. Her brain won't be processing as quickly right now and what might have taken a short time might take longer as the pathways aren't as straight as they were. They'll get there but healing is never quick."

Bishop swallowed and concentrated on the steady beat of her heart against his chest. She was there, she was alive, and they could get through anything else. "I hate this for her."

"I take it this wasn't planned." Savannah sat with her hands in a prayer position between her knees, waiting patiently, and he could see why she was the world-renowned surgeon she was. She had a gentleness about her that was tempered with a sharp mind.

Bishop snorted. "No, most definitely not. Charlie and I are divorced. We had a pretty messy break-up, but the cracks started when we lost our son. He was born at twenty-seven weeks and didn't make it."

"That's a huge strain on a relationship. I'm so sorry."

Bishop took the sympathy and nodded. "We just kind of forgot how to communicate and it tore us apart."

"And she shot you."

Bishop nodded, his chuckle low so as not to disturb Charlie. "She did but the rot had already set in by then. That was a by-product of a woman not coping and going off the rails."

"Still, it was pretty drastic."

"It was but we don't lead normal lives with normal jobs."

"No, that's very true. So this pregnancy must be pretty scary for her and you, especially as it's unplanned."

"It is but I'm excited by it and from the fear I saw in Charlie's eyes, I'm not sure she felt that."

"She needs time to process. Talk to her, give her time, but my advice, and this is from a woman not a doctor, don't pretend you know how it feels. Men and women go through different emotions during pregnancy. She needs you to listen and hear her, not fix it or tell her how she feels. Her hormones will be raging right now which only adds to the stress and emotion."

Bishop nodded again, wondering if he'd done that in the past. "I will, doc."

Savannah stood and glanced at them. "I have a feeling you two will be okay."

"Thanks, Savannah, and thanks for saving her. I don't know what I'd do without her."

"My pleasure."

He could tell by her face that she really meant that. She was humble despite the accolades she had on her office wall.

"Hey, doc, one more question."

"Hmm?"

"Why do you go by doctor when most consultants use Mr or Mrs or Ms?"

A small grin quirked her lips. "I paid thousands and thousands of pounds and even more in blood, sweat, and tears to earn the right to be called doctor. I'm not giving that up for a change in job title. I'm a doctor and proud of it."

"You should be."

"Stop flirting with my wife." A perfectly suited Mark Decker stuck his head in the room and gave him a friendly glare before turning his adoring gaze on his wife.

"You're a lucky man, Mark."

Mark snaked his arm around Savannah's waist and kissed her cheek. "I sure am." He couldn't take his eyes off her and the love was almost uncomfortable but mirrored how he felt about Charlie.

"Get out of here you two. You're making me want to vomit."

"I can prescribe something for that," Savannah quipped but then looked at the woman in his arms. "But I think you have the best medicine right there."

After they left he thought about everything Savannah had said and knew he had to give Charlie space to heal on her own while showing her he was there when she was ready. He just had to pray that she would be ready because the alternative was unthinkable.

Charlie slept fitfully that night and just before dawn he eased his body out from under her and stood looking at her for a few minutes, trying to decide what to do for the best. He didn't want her to feel abandoned, that wasn't what this was. He wanted her to have the space to heal and come to terms with everything.

"I can feel you staring." Blue eyes, with more brightness in them, looked at him before she tried to sit up.

Bishop leaned in and helped her get comfortable. "I was just deciding whether to go get breakfast or not."

Charlie eyed him carefully. "No, you weren't."

Bishop shook his head and shoved his hands in his pockets, so he didn't try and reach for her. "No, I wasn't."

"Talk to me, Noah. Tell me how you feel."

Bishop sank to the chair as she looked at him. "Honestly?"

"Yes, we haven't had enough of that. We need brutal honesty."

"I'm excited, terrified, worried, shocked. I want this baby with you so much, but I'm scared shitless that something might happen again and I'm not sure I could handle it. I'm worried about you, physically and emotionally. I'm in love with you and this baby so hard it makes me feel weak and yet I don't want to push any of that on to you."

Charlie linked her fingers through his. "I love you, Noah." His eyes caught on hers and he felt the blow before it hit. "But I just don't know if I can do this. Losing Freddie broke something inside me, and you ended up hurt because of it. That's a stain on my soul I can't get rid of and I don't want to be the person who hurts you again."

Bishop wanted to beg her, to fall to his knees and promise her anything if she didn't leave him but that wasn't a basis for a future.

Letting her go, he backed up a bit as his heart began to crack in his chest. "I understand." He didn't. He wanted to bellow at the world and rail at her, but he couldn't because he knew she was hurting as much as he was.

"I need to get my head straight." She pointed at the bandages on her head which covered the shaved patch of her skull where Savannah had removed the bullet and saved her life. "Literally."

"Yeah, that's sensible." He needed to get out of there before he broke down and cried like a freaking baby.

"I'm not saying no to a future together, Noah. I just think I need to figure out where I went wrong and see if I can fix that before I try again. Failing for a second time with you would ruin us both and I don't want that."

"I'm going to go. Head back to Longtown and catch up on some work. I missed a lot being here, but when you decide, I'll be waiting."

He saw tears fill her eyes and wanted to go and fix it, to make it right for her. To tell her he had a right to be involved in the choice about their child, but ultimately he wasn't sure he did. It was her body and although it almost brought him to his knees to consider, her right to decide if she continued her pregnancy. He loved her so he had to let her find a way to be her own hero as much as it killed him.

"Be safe, Noah."

"You, too."

Turning, he pushed through the doors and saw Reaper leaning against the wall, boot pressed against the paintwork. Seeing his face, Reaper stepped forward as if he was about to catch him as he staggered down the hallway.

"Jesus, what happened." He looked at the door behind him. "Is Charlie okay?"

Bishop caught his hand on the wall and choked out a response. "Yeah, she uh, just needs some time to get her head straight so I'm going to head back to base. Can you keep a close eye on her and make sure she's safe?"

"Yes, of course, anything."

"Thanks, man."

"You gonna be okay?"

Reaper looked like he was seconds away from calling in backup and he couldn't face anyone else right now. "Yeah, yeah. I just need to get back to work and get some rest and food. Watchdog could probably do with some help on the case."

"Alright, if you're sure."

Bishop squeezed his shoulder. "Yep, yep. All good." He faked a smile which felt odd on his face before he turned and walked away. Every footstep he took away from Charlie was like a blade in his gut.

He put in a call to Bás and briefly explained he was headed back, trying to leave out as many details as he could. His boss was good with it and didn't ask many questions and he had a feeling Reaper had probably beaten him to the punch and forewarned him.

The drive in the rental was uneventful but his stomach was rumbling like a thunderstorm, so he hit the indicator and turned off at a service station with a big blinking fast food sign. A greasy burger and fries would hit the spot, and then he'd finish the drive home and hit the sack for a few hours.

Leaving his car, he hit the locks and walked toward the busy services with cars pulling in and out, families going on trips, businessmen talking on their phones, and truckers looking bored as they hung out slightly away from the rest.

His mind was on Charlie and the words she'd said, not in haste or anger but as if she was finally seeing what she needed for herself. He should be happy, but he was miserable. He missed her already. Her smile, her laugh, the scent of jasmine in her hair, everything about her called to him.

It was like being lost and he was rudderless in the open sea, floating and not knowing how to stop it. She was his anchor and he needed her. Perhaps that was why some space to figure it all out was a good idea. He knew a person should never need someone in their life to be able to breathe. As he bit into his burger, tasting nothing, he chewed and knew a healthy relationship involved two people who wanted to be there, not needed to be there.

Scrunching the empty wrapper up he sucked down the last of his coke and carried the trash to the bin. Placing the tray on the top, he was lost in his own world as he headed to the bathroom before he made the rest of his journey home.

Home, a place he knew would feel less because she wasn't there. His head was down as he walked back to his car after doing everything he needed and he didn't see the van race up beside him until it was too late.

Four hooded men grabbed him, shoving a cloth bag over his head as he fought back, catching one with a right hook, and causing a groan and a muttered damn before a right hook sent him to his ass as stars swam and the world went dark.

CHAPTER 25

CHARLIE FELT HER HEART RATE TICK AS THE DOOR TO HER ROOM OPENED, AND then sink when she saw it wasn't Noah.

"How's your pain?" Natalie, the nurse who'd been so sweet, asked.

"Uh, yeah, not too bad considering."

"Considering what you've been through, it's a damn miracle."

"I guess. It's hard to comprehend it all."

"I'm sure it is, but this afternoon we're going to get you up with the physiotherapist and see how your motor skills and mobility are doing. Sometimes after a traumatic brain injury and a coma, it can take the body a little while to remember everything."

Charlie had little energy for that. All she wanted to do was call Noah and tell him she'd made a horrible mistake and needed him. She didn't do any of that though, and later that afternoon she took the first shaky steps since the bullet had powered into her skull.

"Well, done, Charlie. You're doing great," Snow called from the side-lines where she'd positioned herself as her personal cheerleader.

Charlie scowled at the happy woman as sweat ran down her back. "What's with all the smiling?"

Snow cocked her head and grinned even bigger if that were possible. "It's a good day, Charlie. We thought we'd lost you but here you are on your feet."

"Huh, I'm not yours to lose."

As she finally made it to the end of the short walkway the physio-therapist, a strapping man with muscles for days and the demeanour of a medieval torturer, smiled. "Good. Take a rest and get some water."

Charlie tried to look dignified as she sank into the chair exhausted after only a small amount of exercise. Waking up from her coma had felt like rising from a deep sleep, but it was so much worse. Her body seemed to have taken a vacation, her energy, even though she'd been prone for days, seemed zapped.

Snow walked over, handing her the bottle of cold water which Charlie took and drank like it was the answer to every spot of cellulite on her body.

"I get that you don't know us well, Charlie, but when Shadow takes you under their wing, we don't walk away when the tough stuff happens. We don't turn our backs on each other. We're a family."

Charlie blinked back the stupid tears and blamed the hormones and shock in her system for the leaky outburst.

A warm hand covered hers and she looked down at Snow who'd crouched beside her. "I understand you're terrified of what the future holds but you aren't alone. You have me, Lotus, Duchess, Valentina, Watchdog, Bein, and Bás. You have all of us."

Her lips quivered as she tried to swallow the sob that wanted to break free. These people had offered her everything she'd ever wanted, and she was selfishly worrying about herself. "I'm a horrible person."

Snow wrapped an arm around her and gave her a fierce look. "Hey, no, you're not at all."

"I told Noah I wasn't sure if I could keep the baby. If I could take the risk on us again."

"If you were being honest with yourself, you shouldn't be ashamed of that. Putting yourself first isn't a crime."

"I wasn't."

"Wasn't ashamed or wasn't honest?"

"Honest." Her hand went to her flat stomach to the child who grew despite the odds. She already loved this baby with her whole heart and had never considered anything but a future as his or her mother.

"Do you know why you lied to him?"

"Hey, what's this? A mother's meeting?" Lotus strolled through the door with Bein behind her. She saw Bein look her over and seeing the tear stains, begin to back out.

"Hey, where are you going?" Lotus demanded.

Bein waved his hand toward her. "I don't do tears and stuff."

"Pussy," Lotus called to his retreating back. She turned back with a smile on her pouty lips and looked at her and Snow. "So?"

"Charlie was just telling me how overwhelmed she's feeling about the baby and Bishop and everything."

Charlie was trying to process the last few seconds, her mind working slower than she would have liked, but eventually, it caught up with Lotus' comment. "Mother's meeting?" Her eyes moved to Snow who was blushing. "You're pregnant?"

Snow glared at Lotus who shrugged. "I wasn't going to say as it's early and you have enough going on."

"Oh my God, that's wonderful news. I'm so happy for you. Being a mother is the best." Charlie stopped speaking as she realised her gut reaction was joy for her friend and it had been fear for herself. As she now thought of the child she carried though, a radiant warmth filled her. Yes, it was scary as hell, given everything that had happened, but she wanted this baby and she wanted it with Noah beside her. Leaning forward she hugged Snow. "I'm so happy for you."

"See, I told you hiding it was a mistake. You go down, we go down. Something bad happens then we're there to hold you up until you can do it on your own."

Snow's face softened at Lotus' words, said with such a no-nonsense attitude but imbued with a vast amount of love.

"That goes for you too, Miss I'm-a-loner-and-going-to-self-sacrifice-for-the-man-I-love." Lotus pointed a finger at her with a warning look which Charlie knew was her way of showing she cared.

"Help me up." Charlie, exhausted but filled with renewed hope, moved to stand and found a friend on either side holding her up. It was something she'd never had before this network of friends, and she cherished it now. "I need to get myself back to how I was. I need to be fit and strong, so I can be what my child needs."

"Let's do this." Lotus punched the air. "I'm pumped."

Snow rolled her eyes, but she looked equally energised.

After two more laps of the room, the physio gave her one last go before he was pulling the plug, lecturing her about rest being as important as exercise. He was right, she was exhausted, her limbs and body not wanting to work in the same way they had before she was shot, even her thinking was foggy with her losing concentration quickly. It was scary to have to work for the things she'd taken for granted.

"Come on, Charlie, let's do this and get you back to your old self," Lotus called, cheering her on from the uncomfortable orange plastic chairs.

Charlie stilled as a realisation washed over her. She didn't want to get back to her old self. She wanted a new self and she wanted it with Noah if he'd still have her.

"What the hell, Charlie, you look like you might puke." Lotus' eyes went wide as she took a sidestep. "Are you gonna puke?"

Charlie blinked and shook her head a frown on her face. "What? No."

"Then what the hell? Are you feeling ill?" Lotus turned to Snow. "We let her over-do it." Cupping her elbow on each side the women made her sit in the wheelchair they'd used to bring her to the physio wing. Lotus 'drove' the chair like a freaking maniac and Charlie's stomach did roil then.

"Hey, slow down or I will puke."

"Need you back in bed so Savannah can check you out."

"I'm fine."

"Yeah, let the doc be the judge of that."

As she rounded the corner to the side ward where she was currently a reluctant guest, she saw Savannah waiting for them with concern on her face.

"She went all pale and pukey looking," Lotus told her as they helped her back into bed.

"Let's take a look," Savannah said with her calm, authoritative voice.

Charlie sat still, her mind thinking about the things she'd said to Noah before he'd walked away. He'd walked away. Was that because he didn't think she was worth it?

Lotus pointed an accusing finger in her direction. "See, doc, she's doing it again."

"Do you feel any pain or nausea?"

"My head is a little sore but nothing too bad and I'm not nauseous at the moment."

"Were you earlier?" Savannah shone a light in her eyes and checked the bandage on the side of her head where her luscious hair was shaved for the bullet removal. "Well, it all looks good, and I see nothing to concern me. It could be the pregnancy making you nauseous. As I'm sure you're aware, the term morning sickness is a bit of nonsense as it can strike at any time. You had some blood loss, and your body had a trauma so it's not unusual to have your body fight back when it thinks you're overdoing things."

"It's not that, it's Noah."

"Noah?" Savannah, Snow, and Lotus all asked at once.

Charlie grinned despite the situation watching the women tense up as if they were going to war. "I told him to leave, and he left."

"That's good right?" Lotus asked looking to the other two women for help.

"No."

"No."

"I guess."

Snow and Savannah grinned as they shouted no and looked to her for her I guess.

Snow approached the bed and took her hand forcing Charlie to look at her. "You wanted him to stay and fight for you?"

"That's awful of me, right? I shot him and divorced him. Now we're expecting another child together and I send him away saying I don't know what I want." Charlie buried her head in her hands. "I'm such a bitch."

"A bit, yeah," Lotus agreed, and Charlie grinned when Snow glared at her.

"Lotus."

"What?" Lotus threw up her hands. "Bishop loves her, it's clear as the smell of antiseptic in this room. If he could run ahead of her every step and throw rose petals before her feet he would. What more can he do?"

"That may be so, but Charlie is dealing with her own guilt and feeling unworthy."

Charlie pointed at Snow. "Yes! I don't feel worthy of him. He is such a good man, so loving and caring, and when I was pregnant he was so protective and attentive and he still gave me multiple orgasms, even when I was the size of a whale."

"Word." Lotus held her hand up for a high five, which Charlie obliged.

"Of course you're worthy. You, my friend, are a badass. The only person who doesn't see that is you."

Charlie appreciated Lotus' words. But after being rejected by her mother and treated as nothing more than a child allowance cheque that allowed her to buy more booze, and having a father who thought of her as an afterthought but treated his new family like the moon and the stars, it was a hard mindset to let go of.

"My mother was an alcoholic and looking back on it, she probably had multiple mental health diagnoses that were untreated. She'd be okay for a bit and then she'd get real down and go on a bender for weeks, sometimes months. Then she'd promise she was getting better, and it would be okay and then it wasn't. It got so the bad times were more and more until every day was a bad day."

"I'm sorry. That's tough to deal with. What did you do?"

Charlie drew in a long breath. "I hid it all from social services because she told me I owed her. It was my fault my father didn't want us because I was naughty."

Savannah pursed her lips. "How old were you?"

"Around eight. I was a kid so I believed her. My dad wasn't any better. He always made me feel like he didn't want me around in case I infected his new life with my badness."

Snow looked angry. "What a dick."

"Yeah, Noah hates his guts."

"I'm not surprised."

"When my mum died I was almost relieved, but I was an adult, so I joined the army and found a place there. I was good at it, so good I was recruited by MI5. Then I met Noah and, well, you know the rest."

Savannah stepped forward. "Have you ever had therapy?"

Charlie shook her head. "Not really. A little in the hospital when we lost Freddie, but I wasn't up for it. I just wanted it all to go away."

"I think you need some. Noah too. I see a lot of love between you but if you really want this to work, you need to put the past to bed for good."

Charlie dropped her eyes to her hands which were scrunching the bed sheet up before she smoothed it away. "I think you might be right."

Savannah nodded. "Do you know Peyton Lawson?"

Snow and Lotus both nodded but Charlie wasn't aware of her. "No."

"She's a PTSD counsellor. I think she could help. You've been through so much trauma, and you need help unpacking it all and learning to deal with it and heal."

Charlie knew the doctor was right, she just hoped she hadn't ruined her chances with Noah. "I think you're right. Can you give me her card?"

"I can do better than that. We're discharging you this afternoon and sending you back to Longtown if that's what you want. Peyton lives in Hereford and I can arrange for her to call you and you can figure out a meeting."

"I'm going home?"

"Yes." Savannah smiled, responding to the smile on her face. "I'll check on you twice a week, but I do want you to stay at the Shadow compound, so you have people around you and are safe and rested."

Charlie bit her lower lip wondering if that was a good idea. Hadn't she put these people out enough?

"Stop that shit, I can see you're over-thinking this. Noah would want you there and so do we. Bás practically made it mandatory."

"I don't work for Bás."

Lotus chuckled. "Yet."

"Uh, did you forget the bit about me being knocked up?"

"Of course not, but you won't be pregnant forever and you don't have to do fieldwork. Anyway, not my place."

"No, it's not."

They all turned to see Bás standing at the door, arms crossed over his chest, an unreadable expression on his face.

"Shit," Lotus said but shrugged, clearly unconcerned by her boss' expression.

"Can we have the room?" It wasn't really a question and the three women who'd just talked her off the ledge when she needed it left the room.

Charlie was knackered but she watched Bás approach slowly before taking the chair beside the bed.

"Lotus has a big mouth."

Charlie smiled. "She means well."

"She does and she's a damn fine operator, which is why I don't fire her ass."

"Was she right? About you offering me a job?"

"She was, but I have to be honest. I can't lose Bishop either. He needs to be on board with this too."

"I get that. You're his people."

"Well, if you want us we can be yours too. I spoke to him earlier and he informed me he's okay with it."

"He is?" She stopped, wondering if it was before she dropped her shit on him. "We kind of had words."

Bás braced his hands on his knees. "I heard."

"I think I fucked up."

"Maybe, but nothing that can't be fixed, I'm sure."

"I love him."

"No shit, Sherlock. Maybe I was wrong about you being smart 'cos that shit is obvious."

"Hey."

"Listen, Charlie, I don't do lovely dovey shit well, so I'm gonna say my piece and then leave it up to you. Noah loves you and you love him, and I don't mean in a superficial way. What you have is rare and beautiful. Like Snow and Seb, Bein and Aoife, and Reaper and Lucía. We see a lot of bad shit, the worst humanity has to offer, so when you get handed the sunshine you should grab it with both hands and not ask questions."

"Wow, you're sure you're not good at this because that was epic."

Bás rolled his eyes and stood. "You have a job if you want it, in whatever capacity that is and obviously there's no rush. You heal first, then decide if you want a place with Shadow."

"Thank you, Bás, for everything. Helping with Andrea, all of it."

"My pleasure and don't forget without you we wouldn't know Carter Cavendish was involved with Project Cradle, so thank you."

Charlie nodded and relaxed back against the pillows thoroughly wrung out from the emotion and the hard work she'd forced on her body. She had a lot of thinking to do. Resting her hand over her flat tummy, Charlie knew one thing. She wasn't giving up on her and Noah this time.

CHAPTER 26

BISHOP COULD HEAR BICKERING IN HUSHED VOICES WHEN HE WOKE WITH A start. Everything rushed back to him as he sat up quickly, his feet landing on the floor of a living room with lush navy couches and light hardwood floors. On alert, he let his eyes travel the room and didn't see a threat. It was an elegant, classy room in what looked like a modern apartment.

Standing, he listened again to see where the voices were coming from and moving slowly, he stretched his jaw and rubbed the tender spot where someone had punched him so hard it knocked his lights out.

"You didn't need to hit him so hard, asshole."

Bishop frowned, he knew that voice, recognised the annoyed and controlled tone of it.

"He almost kicked me in the crown jewels, and I need those to produce more little princesses for the world to adore."

Liam Hayes! What the fuck?

Bishop ploughed through the door and was confronted with Jack Granger, Liam Hayes, Alex Martinez, Mark Decker, and Calvin Blake, all sitting at the table drinking fucking tea like a bunch of pussies while he slept off his punch to the face.

"Ah, you're awake." Blake stood to grab a mug and began filling it with tea.

"What the fuck is going on? You kidnapped me?" Bishop ran his hands through his hair, pulling at the ends as he tried to figure it all out.

"Here, sit down. And it wasn't a kidnapping, it was an intervention." Jack glared at Liam as he spoke.

"I mean, strictly speaking, it was a kidnapping, boss man," Blake interjected as he placed a mug in front of him at the table and motioned for him to sit.

Bishop sank into the chair because his brain was struggling to keep up with this amount of crazy.

"You're fired, Blake."

"Thanks, boss." Blake seemed to be unconcerned that his boss had just fired him and dunked a biscuit in his tea.

"So wait, you kidnapped me, punched me, and brought me here? Why?"

"Liam punched you. We were trying to do this the easy way but fuck, man, you fought back hard." Alex looked impressed as he curled his lip at Blake dunking his biscuits. "That's a disgusting habit."

"Hey, do not yuck my yum until you try it."

"Never. I just don't get the British sometimes."

"Says the man who thinks snails are a delicacy."

"They are."

"Gross," Decker interjected.

"Can we please focus and you tell me why the hell I'm here and not on the motorway heading home?"

Jack sat back and looked at Liam again. "The floor is yours, oh wise one."

Liam grinned and cocked his head. "Thank you for finally acknowledging that." He turned to Bishop who was losing patience fast. These men were top-notch operators tasked with keeping Queen Lydia safe and yet here they were acting like a bunch of geriatrics at Parish Council meeting. "You were being stupid, so we thought you needed some wisdom from five happily married men."

"Stupid, how? And why does your marital status matter?"

Alex frowned. "How hard did you hit him, Liam?"

"Not that hard. He should be catching on quicker."

"Look, what dickhead here is saying is that when Charlie kicked you out and said she needed space, she didn't mean it."

"Wait, how the hell do you know she kicked me out?"

"Reaper," Jack answered, stealing a biscuit from Blake who grinned and raised his eyebrows at Alex.

"Reaper?"

"Yeah, he heard Charlie give you the heave-ho."

"She didn't give me the heave-ho, she asked for space so I'm giving her that."

Decker looked at Jack. "You sure he worked for MI5 'cos he doesn't seem to catch on real quick."

"Yeah, Will checked him out and Lopez verified."

"Huh."

"So all this is because you think I should, what? Have stayed where she didn't want me?"

"Yes!" they all yelled.

"You're all fucking crazy."

"I can verify that isn't the case," Decker, the profiler, answered. "Look, Charlie asked for space, but she just got shot in the head and she's pregnant and scared and she's carrying so much guilt over shooting your ugly ass, that it's a wonder she can walk straight."

"I've told her I don't blame her for that."

Decker sighed. "Look, man, when I realised I was head over ass for Savannah, do you know what I did?" He didn't give Bishop chance to answer before he spoke again. "I ran as far away as I could. I felt so awful for loving her after losing my wife and son."

Bishop sipped his tea which was just how he liked it, strong and sweet. A bit like his wife. "I'm sorry, I didn't know. That's hard, man."

Decker nodded. "It was, but I learned that love is the only thing that matters sometimes, and that letting guilt keep taking from you isn't a good way to honour the memory of those we lost."

Bishop swallowed the lump in his throat at the emotion in the other man's eyes. "I should have been home and then she wouldn't have climbed that damn chair."

"And you may still have lost your son. It's tragic and devastating but awful shit happens."

"That doesn't explain why you punched me in the face and threw a bag over my head."

"Because your guilt over not being home when she fell is why you turned and ran away so easily."

Bishop pushed his chair back and stood abruptly. "I did not run the fuck away."

Decker stood. "Yeah, you did. You know for a fact nobody has ever fought for Charlie and yet still you ran."

"She shot me. She doesn't want me."

"Bullshit, she loves you but between the pair of you and losing your son, you lost your way. You need to pull your head out of your ass and fight for her. Show her she's worth it, that you don't blame her and won't run when she tries to push you away."

Bishop felt overwhelmed with the weight of the truth being laid on him. "Why are you doing this?"

"Because most of us fucked up too, and we don't want to see you make the same mistake."

Bishop sank into the chair his body heavy. "How do I fix this?"

Liam clapped his hands. "Yes, now we're talking. I have so many ideas."

"Shut up, Liam. This is not a fucking rom-com."

"He's right, this is going to take something big for Charlie to understand I won't be letting her go no matter how much she pushes me away."

"Well, I happen to know Bás has arranged for her to be transported back to Shadow HQ for her recovery."

"He has? When?"

Jack looked at his watch. "About an hour's time."

"I need to go."

"Hey, slow your roll." Jack raised his palm and patted the air for him to calm it. "We can call Gunner to pick us up in the helo, so you have plenty of time."

"Cool, thanks. And thanks for this. I know we don't work alongside you guys a lot but it's a privilege to be part of Shadow and that's because of you guys."

"Aww, shucks, he's gonna make me cry," Blake joked and then grabbed Bishop in a headlock. "Just fix this shit."

"I'm gonna."

As they took the short flight back to base landing on the Black Mountains helipad for the rescue centre, his mind was going full throttle on how he could win back his wife.

He headed to his apartment not stopping to see Watchdog, who'd already made it back after visiting Charlie. Inside, he went to the box he kept full of all the things he couldn't part with after his marriage ended.

Sitting on the bed he took a breath and opened it. On the top was his marriage certificate, signed by them both, her swirling cursive so different to his blocky signature. Underneath were photos from that day. Of him and Charlie and the few guests they'd had, drinking and having fun. They looked so young, so carefree and happy, and he wished he could go back and warn that young couple of the pitfalls they faced.

He picked up his favourite photo of them, her smiling at him as he kissed her rounded belly. Her hand in his hair, the other cradling their son. A pang of pain knotted his gut, and he laid the picture aside. Seeing the glint of the wedding band she'd given him, he picked it up. He hadn't worn it a lot because of his job. In their line of work having a wife was a risk. He felt the warm weight of the titanium band and pushed it onto his finger over the knuckle.

It felt strange and yet something settled inside him. A rightness that he hadn't felt before as if the timing was right this time, and it hadn't been before. Sliding the ring off, he closed the box. He knew what he had to do, but first, he had a call to make.

An hour later he walked into Peyton Lawson's office and spilled every single secret he had. No matter how sordid or difficult it was, he let it all out. If he wanted Charlie he had to be the man she needed, and that didn't involve a boat load of guilt.

As he left with the homework she'd given him for the week, he felt hopeful. A text telling him Charlie was on her way made him still and turn the car around and drive into town. He needed to show her this was it for him, and that she was everything to him.

CHAPTER 27

WHEN THEY'D GOTTEN BACK TO SHADOW HQ, CHARLIE HAD BEEN SO exhausted she couldn't even keep her eyes open while Bien's fiancée Aoife checked her blood pressure. Apparently, she was training to be a nurse and Savannah had given her instructions on what to check and when and she was taking it very seriously. She'd woken her at seven that morning to check her over and give her some medication for the pain. Savannah had assured her it was safe for the baby and she trusted the woman who'd saved her life.

"Now you can get dressed but you're not to do anything without help, and I mean nothing," Aoife warned, the red-haired beauty pointing a finger at her and trying to look frightening.

"I won't. I have no plans to jeopardise my recovery."

"Good, someone will be by with breakfast shortly."

Charlie nodded as Aoife left with a secret smile on her lips as if she knew something Charlie didn't.

A shower sounded wonderful, but Charlie knew she should wait until someone was with her. Guilt that she was causing so much work for these people made her want to try it alone, but she knew that would get her a lecture from Lotus, and nobody wanted that.

Her door opening had her gasping slightly at seeing Noah in the doorway looking devastatingly handsome in old, worn jeans and a black t-shirt, the tattoo on his biceps just visible.

"Good morning. I'll be your nurse for the day."

"Nurse?"

"Well, more of a skivvy, so whatever you need I'm your man."

"I need a shower."

Charlie saw the heat flicker in his eyes as they raked over her body and felt the twinge of desire swirl through her body.

"I can help, or I can call one of the girls if you don't feel comfortable with me."

Charlie snorted. "Come on, Noah, you've seen and touched every inch of me. If I don't feel comfortable with you then I won't with anyone."

He nodded and approached slowly as if she were a skittish animal about to bolt. He looked unsure of himself, and she hated that.

When he was within touching distance she reached for him, and he opened his arms as she stepped into them. A feeling of coming home wrapped around her and she let him hold her. Noah would always be home for her. He was the man who'd seen her at her worst, who'd loved her when she didn't deserve it, and she needed him to know how much he meant to her and apologise. "I'm so sorry, Noah."

He pulled away and frowned as he looked at her intently. "Don't apologise. I should've stayed and I didn't." He led her toward the couch and sank down with her still in his arms. "I ran when you pushed me because I still feel like I failed you."

"No."

He put a finger over her lips, and she noticed a mark on his wedding finger. Grasping his wrist, she held his hand still so she could look at it. In a band around the base of his finger was a new tattoo. Hope bloomed in her chest, and she wondered if she was silly to read something into this, but when she lifted her eyes to see him grinning his swoon-worthy smile at her, she let that fledgling hope soar.

"What does it say?" She knew it was a word but not the language it was written in and couldn't read it.

"It says *Charlie*."

She blinked fast, tears hitting her eyes as fast as she could clear them. "What?"

"I know I ran, but since the day we met, I have been yours, heart and soul. It doesn't matter if you don't want me, because in my heart I'm married to you, Charlie, and always will be. I'm not going anywhere, ever. I love you and no matter what you decide, that won't change."

"You love me?"

"I have always, and will always love you, Charlie."

"But I sent you away and I said.... Oh, God, I suggested I wouldn't have our baby."

"I won't say that wasn't hard to hear, because it was, but whatever you decide won't affect how much I love you."

"I was never going to do anything but keep this baby. I was just pushing you away."

"And I should've seen that."

"No, Noah." She cupped his cheek. "I should have. It's not your job to second guess my crazy."

"It is because that's what we do for those we love. We see when they can't."

"I see a man who loves hard, who carries too much weight on his sexy shoulders, and who I never want to be apart from ever again."

"This mean you're gonna marry me again?"

A tear slid down her cheek, followed by another until she couldn't breathe, and he held her while she cried and let the pain of the past go. "Yes, yes I want to marry you again, although in my heart I was never divorced."

"I'm glad you feel that way because when Watchdog checked, he found out that you never filed the paperwork for our divorce, so we're actually still married."

"No!"

"Yes, you're still Mrs Bishop."

"I wouldn't want to be anything else."

Noah's face softened. "I love you so much, Charlie, and I promise you this time it will be different. I'm seeing Peyton Lawson to help get my head straight and I'm going to be the man you need."

"No way."

Noah frowned as his fingers caressed her neck. "No?"

"I have an appointment with Peyton too, she is going to recommend a therapist for me who deals with infant death. I have too much baggage and I'm not bringing it with me this time."

"Who suggested her?"

"Savannah Decker. Why?"

"Sneaky bastards. Mark Decker suggested her to me. I guess they all want us to be together."

"None more than me, Noah. I love you and I'm terrified by this pregnancy, but I know we'll get through it together this time."

His lips captured hers in a passionate kiss and all of the hurt and pain seemed to disappear as desire took over. Lifting her hand she stroked his jaw and he winced.

Looking closer she saw a bruise under the stubbled jaw she loved so much. "What happened?"

"It's a long story."

Charlie wriggled, feeling the ridge of his hard cock beneath her thighs. "Well, how about you tell me after my shower."

His hands landed on her hips and stilled her. "Baby, I want nothing more than to plunge my cock inside you and fuck you until we're both screaming but you're not allowed until Savannah signs off on sex being permitted."

Charlie poked out her tongue. "Spoilsport."

Lifting her in his arms he carried her out of her apartment and next door into his, walking straight toward the shower.

"What are you doing?"

His fingers skimmed her ribs as he drew the tee overhead and threw it to the floor and knelt and began to run the bath. His shirt went next, and she watched with hungry eyes as his muscles rippled, tantalising her.

"I didn't say we couldn't have fun, but we need to be careful and conserve your energy." Dropping his jeans, he fell to his knees and pulled the pyjama pants down with her underwear tangled with them.

Her legs shook, and she knew it was from need, not weakness caused by her being shot.

As the room filled with steam and the scent of lavender, Noah got into the bath with her and made her lean back against his chest. His hard erection pressed into her back as the warm water lapped over her skin. His hands lathered in body wash smoothed over her shoulders and down her arms where he linked their fingers. "I missed this."

Charlie had no desire to play games, so she answered honestly. "Me too. Do you remember when we stayed up all night talking on the phone just because we couldn't bear to be apart?"

"I still have one of your voice mails on my phone."

His admission startled her, and she tipped her head back to look at him. "You do?"

"Yes. You called when I was meeting a contact and it went to voicemail. You told me you were making roast potatoes and chicken and if I made it home in time I could have you for dessert."

Charlie bit her lip. "I remember that. We ended up having each other for starters and cold chicken and potatoes later that night."

Noah let her hands go as they slid over her hips to her tummy. Reverently he held his palm over where their child grew. The room was charged with so much energy, desire, love, and sadness but mostly hope.

Charlie covered his hand with her own. "I know this was far from planned but this baby feels destined, somehow. Does that sound silly?"

She felt Noah's head shake behind her, his stubble catching her hair. "Not at all. I think this baby was meant to bring us back to each other and anchor us."

"Or force us to get our shit together."

His chuckle tickled her neck and Charlie felt her nipples bead as they poked above the warm water.

"Fuck, you're beautiful."

"Oh, the bandage is the clincher I'm sure."

His fingers lifted her face towards his with infinite care. "Everything you do is beautiful to me."

Charlie believed him too, she could see it in the stormy swirl of his eyes, felt it as he kissed her, his tongue tangling with hers in a kiss that was drugging. Making her mind forget anything but him.

Noah cupped her breasts, his thumb and finger teasing her nipple until she was gasping for more. Needy for him to make her feel human again. "You want to come, baby?"

"Yes." Her words rushed out of her, and he smirked, a sexy image that went straight to her pussy.

Noah worked her over, his fingers toying with her nipples, pulling and teasing until she thought she might combust. Then when she thought she couldn't take anymore, he slid a finger through the folds of her pussy, skimming her clit and entering her as she gripped his arm.

Her husband, the man she'd never stopped loving, fucked her with his hand while telling her how sexy she was, how beautiful, how much he adored her and Charlie came with his name on her lips, knowing that the future, no matter how scary, would be filled with love because of this man.

EPILOGUE

CHARLIE BIT HER BOTTOM LIP AS SHE WAITED FOR THE ANAESTHETIST TO come and give her the epidural. "I feel like I'm wimping out doing it this way."

Noah wrapped his arm tighter around her shoulders, his other hand smoothing over her very round belly. "Are you kidding? How can you say a C-section is cheating? It's a massive surgery and there's no cheating in childbirth."

Charlie stroked his cheek, smooth from the shave he'd insisted on this morning before they'd come to the hospital to have their daughter by C-section.

"I know. I just hadn't planned her to come out through the sunroof."

"Sunroof?" Noah laughed, his breath tickling her ear. "None of this has been planned, including little miss here being upside down."

"Breech, Noah, she's breech."

"Whatever. All I'm saying is however it happens, it was meant to be that way. As long as I have you and her in my arms tonight, I'll be a happy man."

"Are you scared?" She hated admitting her own fears, but the last eight months had shown her that showing weakness and allowing people to help when you needed them was a good thing.

"Fucking terrified, and excited, and in love, and unworthy. I can't even describe everything I'm feeling, Charl, but I know whatever I feel I want it with you beside me."

"I love you, Noah Bishop."

"I love you, Mrs Bishop."

The door to the hospital room opened and Savannah Decker and another doctor walked inside. "Good morning, both." She picked up the chart from the bottom of the bed and scanned it with proficient eyes. "Are you ready to meet your baby?"

"So ready."

Savannah smiled at them with warmth. "And are you certain you want me to deliver this baby? I can have a wonderful gynae consultant I know up here in minutes."

"No, we want you." Savannah had saved her life and there was nobody they trusted more with the delivery of their child.

"Well, I'm honoured. Dr March is going to give you the epidural and then we'll get started."

Charlie felt her stomach swim with butterflies, her heart racing like a runaway train as the room filled with surgical staff and two paediatric doctors ready to step in and check their baby once she was born. Noah was gowned up so he could hold her hand and be part of this with her, and she couldn't imagine doing this with anyone else.

She curled around a pillow and Noah sat in front of her as the doctor gave her the epidural into her spine.

"You got this, Charlie."

Looking at the ceiling she listened as the doctors began, Noah murmuring beside her as he watched over the sheet they'd erected to stop her from seeing the surgery.

"Almost there, Charlie. I can the baby's feet."

A smile spread across her face as she glanced at her husband to see tears in his eyes and in that second, she wasn't sure she could love him more.

The feeling of pulling and pushing in her tummy made a wave of nausea sweep over her.

"Doc, she looks like she might puke."

Noah rubbed her hand as something was injected into her IV and the feeling of nausea faded. A cry tore through the air and then Savannah was holding up a tiny, perfect baby who was red and screaming her beautiful lungs out.

A sob escaped her as emotion and love overwhelmed her and she glanced at Noah to see tears streaming down his face. He squeezed her hand as they watched their daughter being whisked over to the incubator and cleaned off, still making her objections to the abrupt change of scenery known.

"She looks good. I'm just going to fix this all up while they weigh her."

"Is she okay?"

Noah looked toward Savannah who nodded. "Perfectly fine. Can you hear the lungs on that child?"

Moments later the nurse was handing their daughter to Noah, who took her in his arms as if she was the most delicate, breakable glass. He cradled her close as he brought her to Charlie's eye line.

"She's perfect."

He dropped a kiss on her head, his smile so bright it lit the room. "I won't let anyone hurt you, princess, not ever."

It was an hour later once she'd been sewn back together and was still a little groggy from the morphine that she finally got to hold her daughter.

"I can't believe she's here."

"What shall we call her?" During her pregnancy, they hadn't taken a second for granted so names were put on hold until they saw her.

"What about Iris?"

Charlie smiled through the exhaustion hitting her. "I like that."

"It means rainbow and she's ours."

"That's beautiful, Noah. How about Iris Winifred after Freddie too? I want to honour him and not forget that we've been blessed twice over."

"Perfect. Iris Winifred."

Noah stroked Iris' cheek as she fed. "You were amazing, Charlie. I didn't think I could be more in awe of you but every day you surprise me and show me how lucky I am to have you in my life."

"I was thinking earlier how I couldn't love you more and then I saw you with her and knew I'd spend my life loving you more each day."

His lips met hers as he cupped her face. It was sweet and beautiful. They were a family now, but she'd come to realise over the last nine months that family wasn't blood, it was stepping up and being there at the worst and the best moments.

"You should go see them. They'll be chomping at the bit for news."

Noah nodded and stood, taking a sleepy Iris, who seemed milk drunk from her arms. "I won't be long."

"It's fine. I'm probably going to catch a nap."

He bent and kissed her and she sighed, knowing she had her happy ending with the promise of beauty and joy ahead of her. It wouldn't all be sunshine and roses but now she had the tools, and more importantly, the people to help her cope with anything life threw her way.

Pushing through the door from the private room into the lounge where his friends were waiting for news, Bishop felt pride and love so strong he thought he'd choke on it. His eyes never wanted to leave Iris but as he dragged them away, he saw every single member of Shadow Elite and their partners waiting for him.

"Guys, I'd like you all to meet Iris Winifred Bishop."

Instantly he was surrounded, everyone trying to get a look at the first Shadow baby to grace the team and change the dynamic. Before they'd fought for justice, and now each of them knew they fought for family too.

"She's so beautiful, Bish." Snow, who looked like she was ready to drop her own bundle of joy any second, kissed his cheek.

"This will be you soon."

Sebastian wrapped his arm around his petite wife and kissed her head. "Two weeks until the due date."

"I need this baby out now. I can't see my feet."

"How is Charlie doing?"

Watchdog and Charlie had become close, like siblings in some ways and she'd spent a lot of time with him during her pregnancy while he was on jobs and he'd been glad of it. "She was amazing. So calm and brave. She's tired but I guess that's our new normal for a while."

Lotus grinned. "Put me down for babysitting when you need a break."

"Yep, me too," Val added.

"I'm not offering my services for nappies, but I'll help with cooking or whatever other shit you need," Titan offered as the others joined in, not wanting to be left out.

"Thank you, guys, that means a lot to us."

Bás rested a hand on Bishop's shoulder. "You're family and so is she, and we look after family."

Bishop nodded because he couldn't speak past the lump in his throat. These men and women had saved him in his darkest hour and continued to be there every minute of the day.

"We should let you get back to Charlie." Duchess stroked a finger over Iris' blanket-covered feet. "Do you need us to do anything at your place before you come home?"

They'd bought a house in the village, one that Miss Rose, who'd predicted he'd need to forgive before he could move on, had suggested. She'd turned up at the Mountain Rescue Centre and told him she needed a lift and had taken him to a house just outside the village. It was a 1930s property with four bedrooms, three bathrooms, and a large garden and driveway. It had needed remodelling but nothing huge and he'd fallen in love with the property.

Lucky for him so had Charlie and they'd bought it and renovated it and had moved in just last month. It was home, where he and Charlie would raise their family and if Miss Rose was right, more children in the future.

"How are you at building a crib?"

"I can do that," Hurricane said with a wink.

"Thanks, man."

"Of course."

Making his way back to Charlie he found her fast asleep in the huge bed. Placing Iris in her bassinet, he pulled the blanket over her tiny body and climbed in beside Charlie. Adjusting her so she was in his arms, he kissed her as she startled awake.

"Iris?"

"Is fast asleep."

His hands moved over her settling her worries as she sagged against him again. "I thought it was a dream."

"No, she's not a dream. Well, she is, but not like that."

Charlie nestled into his arms but they both kept their eyes on the crib which held their entire world. "What did the guys say?"

"Let's just say our daughter has stolen more than just our hearts today. I have a feeling she has a bunch of protective uncles willing to go to jail to protect her from any punks who mess with her."

"Ha, I'd be more scared of all those aunts if I was any boyfriend."

"Argh, no. Don't say the word boyfriend. She's going to join a nunnery."

"Yeah, good luck with that, Noah."

"I love her so much."

"I know. It's crazy how all of a sudden your heart just triples in size for this tiny human who you don't even know yet."

"I know she's half you and that's enough for me."

"Thank you, Noah, for loving me, for forgiving me."

"Thank you for loving me so hard you shot me."

Charlie pinched his nipple.

He rubbed the abused flesh. "Hey, what was that for?"

"For being an idiot."

"Fair point. You're still going to pay for that when you're all healed."

"Hey, don't be cute when I'm all drugged."

"Okay."

As Charlie slept he kept watch over his girls and vowed he'd protect and love them until the day he took his last breath.

This might be the happy ever after for Bishop and Charlie, but for a sneak peek of Duchess and Gideon's story, read on.

SNEAK PEEK: SHADOW FIVE
DUCHESS AND GIDEON

"Good morning, Mr Cavendish. Here are your papers for the day."

Duchess handed Damon Cavendish the papers as she did every morning since she'd gone undercover as his secretary to get more dirt on Carter Cavendish and his mother.

"Thank you. We have a meeting in the boardroom in five minutes."

Damon looked annoyed and instantly Duchess went on alert. "There's nothing in the diary, Mr Cavendish."

Damon glanced around the outer sanctum of his office space which had been her home for six months. "My brother called it last minute."

"I see. Will I be needed?"

"Yes."

Damon went into his office and closed the door on her, leaving her to wonder what the hell was going on, and more importantly, why Damon looked so pissed off? He was usually calm. The three brothers were very different, yet they all had the same gorgeous dark looks and sexy build. Carter was the half-sibling to Gideon and Damon. Carter was the man she was after, who she was sure

214

was involved in Project Cradle. He ran a billion-pound empire on illegal drugs, human trafficking, and any other manner of things. Damon was the frontman, who attended the galas and events as the face of the business. He dated beautiful women, charmed investors, and was an astute and well-respected barrister who handled a lot of pro-bono work. He was a good man and had become a solid friend to her as they'd worked together to take down Carter and remove the stink from the Cavendish empire once and for all.

Then there was Gideon, gorgeous, sexy, grumpy, aloof, and cold. He was a genius with business and there wasn't a deal that went down without his knowledge or approval. He was the reason the legal side of the business was becoming more successful than the illegal side. He was the man she hated with a passion and wanted with a desperation she couldn't fathom. He plagued her nightmares and her dreams in equal measure.

He was the man who could get her killed because he was distracting and dangerous to her equilibrium. Which was why she worked for Damon on this project. They both knew why she was really there and they wanted Shadow's help but Duchess knew working alongside a man who could make her forget who she was would be a disaster.

"Time to go."

So deep in thought that she hadn't heard Damon approach, she jumped up and raced after him. Her skin itched from the make-up she wore to hide her tattoos in the stuffy environment, but it was more they'd draw attention to her that she didn't need. Mousy and plain was what she was going for in a knee-length skirt and a high neck blouse, little make-up, red lips her only nod to her real self. Her dark hair was in a tight bun at the base of her neck, which gave her a raging headache by the day's end. It was so far from the real her as to be laughable, but a great cover.

Entering the large conference room, she saw it was empty. The glass table held enough seats for every board member and overlooked Canary Wharf in London's business district. The view was beautiful, even on a dreary day like today.

She rounded on her fake boss, hands on hips. "What's going on, Damon?"

"What's going on is that there's going to be a slight shake-up in personnel."

Duchess turned to see Gideon stalking toward her like a predator about to take a bite out of some poor unsuspecting deer. He wore a three-piece suit in charcoal grey, a dark blue shirt, and a black tie. He looked deadly and her body wanted to swoon at the sight of him.

Straightening her spine she ignored her erect nipples and hoped he wouldn't notice, refusing to give in to the desire to cross her arms over her chest.

He glanced down and smirked before brushing past her.

"Damon, I'm in need of a PA. Mine quit and as you're in court for the next six weeks or so, I'd like Miss Benassi to stand in until I can arrange someone else."

Damon glanced at her and she glared at him, daring him to agree. He shrugged and turned to his brother. "It's not really up to me, is it? You know the score, brother."

"Then that's settled. Miss Benassi, please move your belonging to my office immediately."

Gideon spun as if to leave and she lost her cool. "I don't think so. I'm here to do a job and you know for a fact that's not to be your Girl Friday."

Gideon pinned her with a glare as he strode toward her, stopping mere centimetres from her. She could smell his aftershave, something spicy that reminded her of sweaty sex and champagne.

He looked down at her. Even in her heels, she couldn't match his six-foot-four height. "I'm quite aware of why you're here."

"Then you know I'm perfectly fine where I am."

"On the contrary, Miss Benassi. You need access to Carter, and I need a PA. If I don't get that, you'll no longer have our help in this matter."

"Gideon! Don't be rash. We need her."

Gideon held up his hand to his brother, who swore. "We don't need her, but I'll agree she's helpful."

Damon threw up his hands and walked toward the door of the conference room, about to leave her alone to deal with the devil.

Gideon's gaze swept over her body making it clear what he thought her uses were. This arrogant prick was pushing her buttons trying to get a reaction. Well, she'd give him one. "It's fine, Damon. I can work with Gideon for six weeks, but I have my own terms."

Her friend held her eyes a moment longer before he nodded and left the room.

Gideon's eyes flickered as they dropped to her lips. "What would those be?"

"I want more access to Carter. I want to be seen at the galas, the dinners. I want to know everything about his habits outside of work and I want to see him interact with his mother and your father."

"Done."

Gideon smiled and it looked more like a threat than a happy emotion. "Please find a more appropriate work wardrobe, Miss Benassi. I can see your nipples through that blouse."

With that, he turned and left the conference room, and she fought the urge to go after him and show him just how he'd underestimated her. A smile spread over her lips as she thought of all the things she'd do to make him pay for his arrogance.

WANT A FREE SHORT STORY?

Sign up for Maddie's Newsletter using the link below and receive a free copy of the short story, Fortis: Where it all Began.

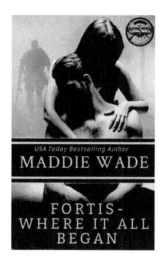

When hard-nosed SAS operator, Zack Cunningham is forced to work a mission with the fiery daughter of the American General, sparks fly. As those heated looks turn into scorching hot stolen kisses, a forbidden love affair begins that neither had expected.

Just as life is looking perfect disaster strikes and Ava Drake is left wondering if she will ever see the man she loves again.

https://dl.bookfunnel.com/cyrjtv3tta

BOOKS BY MADDIE WADE

FORTIS SECURITY

Healing Danger (Dane and Lauren)

Stolen Dreams (Nate and Skye)

Love Divided (Jace and Lucy)

Secret Redemption (Zack and Ava)

Broken Butterfly (Zin and Celeste)

Arctic Fire (Kanan and Roz)

Phoenix Rising (Daniel and Megan)

Nate & Skye Wedding Novella

Digital Desire (Will and Aubrey)

Paradise Ties: A Fortis Wedding Novella (Jace and Lucy & Dane and Lauren)

Wounded Hearts (Drew and Mara)

Scarred Sunrise (Smithy and Lizzie)

Zin and Celeste: A Fortis Family Christmas

Fortis Boxset 1 (Books 1-3)

Fortis Boxset 2 (Books 4-7.5

EIDOLON

Alex

Blake

Reid

Liam

Mitch

Gunner

Waggs

Jack

Lopez

Decker

SHADOW ELITE

Guarding Salvation

Innocent Salvation

Royal Salvation

Stolen Salvation

Lethal Salvation

WOMEN OF DECEPTION (ZENOBI)

Palace of Betrayal (September 2022)

ALLIANCE AGENCY SERIES (CO-WRITTEN WITH INDIA KELLS)

Deadly Alliance

Knight Watch

Hidden Obsession

Lethal Justice

Innocent Target

Power Play

Until Forever (Shane and Emme Wedding Novella)

RYOSHI DELTA (PART OF SUSAN STOKER'S POLICE AND FIRE: OPERATION ALPHA WORLD)

Condor's Vow

Sandstorm's Promise

Hawk's Honor

Omega's Oath

Lyric's Truth

TIGHTROPE DUET

Tightrope One

Tightrope Two

ANGELS OF THE TRIAD

01 Sariel

OTHER WORLDS

About the Author

Contact Me

If stalking an author is your thing and I sure hope it is then here are the links to my social media pages.

If you prefer your stalking to be more intimate, then my group Maddie's Minxes will welcome you with open arms.

General Email: info.maddiewade@gmail.com
Email: maddie@maddiewadeauthor.co.uk
Website: http://www.maddiewadeauthor.co.uk
Facebook page: https://www.facebook.com/maddieuk/
Facebook group: https://www.facebook.com/groups/546325035557882/
Goodreads: https://www.goodreads.com/author/show/14854265.Maddie_Wade
Bookbub: https://partners.bookbub.com/authors/3711690/edit
Twitter: @mwadeauthor
Pinterest: @maddie_wade
Instagram: Maddie Author

Printed in Great Britain
by Amazon